Dishonour in Camp 133

Also by Wayne Arthurson

The Traitors of Camp 133

Dishonour in Camp 133

A Sergeant Neumann Mystery

Wayne Arthurson

Dishonour in Camp 133
© Wayne Arthurson 2021

Published by Ravenstone an imprint of Turnstone Press
Artspace Building, 206-100 Arthur Street
Winnipeg, MB. R3B 1H3 Canada
www.TurnstonePress.com

Turnstone Press gratefully acknowledges the assistance of the Canada Council for the Arts, the Manitoba Arts Council, the Government of Canada through the Canada Book Fund, and the Province of Manitoba through the Book Publishing Tax Credit and the Book Publisher Marketing Assistance Program.

This novel is a work of fiction. Names, characters, places and incidents are either the product of the author's imagination or are used fictitiously, and any resemblance to actual persons living or dead, events or locales, is entirely coincidental.

Printed and bound in Canada by Friesens for Turnstone Press.

Library and Archives Canada Cataloguing in Publication

Title: Dishonour in Camp 133 / Wayne Arthurson.
Other titles: Dishonour in Camp One Hundred Thirty-Three
Names: Arthurson, Wayne, 1962- author.
Description: Series statement: A Sergeant Neumann mystery
Identifiers: Canadiana (print) 20210289481 | Canadiana
   (ebook) 20210289511 | ISBN 9780888016218 (softcover) |
   ISBN 9780888016225 (EPUB) | ISBN 9780888016249 (PDF)
Classification: LCC PS8551.R888 D57 2021 | DDC C813/.6—dc23

To Auni and Vianne

Dishonour in Camp 133

Lethbridge, Canada

December 1, 1944

1.

Chef Schlipal was slumped over his regular table in Mess #3, a knife in his back. Several lines of blood trailed down the chef's apron and pants, gathering into a small, congealed puddle. The scent of shit lingered in the air.

Sergeant August Neumann stood about two metres away from Schlipal, hands behind his back, rocking on his heels. Schlipal's table was in the back of the Mess, near the entrance to the kitchen. His head and shoulders rested on a mess of paper scattered across the table. None of the papers had fallen to the floor, but a can full of cigarette butts had spilled out, seemingly knocked over by his left arm. At first glance, it looked as if Schlipal had just decided to take a snooze at his desk after determining the menu for that day's breakfast.

But there was the issue of the knife in his back, which Neumann found troubling. The blade of the knife had been completely embedded in Schlipal, with the handle, and its knuckle guard, protruding from his back.

"Is he dead?" asked Corporal Dieter Knaup, a 21-year-old prisoner who stood behind Neumann, holding a pencil in his right hand that was poised over a notebook that he held with his left. Knaup was tall and muscular with a pimply face that made him look like an adolescent school boy. The brown rucksack draped over his left shoulder only re-enforced that look. But Knaup, like the majority of the prisoners in Camp 133, had seen plenty of combat. So while he looked young, there was weariness around his eyes.

"He is most definitely dead, Corporal Knaup. There's no doubt about that."

Knaup scribbled in his notebook. "What shall we do now?" he asked.

"We are doing what we are supposed to be doing."

Knaup scribbled but then stopped and looked up. "And what is that?" he asked after a moment of thought.

Neumann turned to look at Knaup. The corporal dropped his head and stepped back in deference to the look. "I'm sorry, Sergeant Neumann. Unlike Corporal Aachen, I'm not versed in these matters."

Neumann chuckled. "That's okay, Knaup. Not many people are versed in the matters of murder. I'm pretty sure that Corporal Aachen would ask a very similar question."

"So you believe it is murder, then?" Knaup asked, eyes looking up at the sergeant but head still down.

"Yes, the presence of the knife makes that obvious."

Knaup blushed and dropped his gaze. "Sorry, Sergeant. I didn't mean … of course I saw the knife."

Neumann sighed. "Snap out of it, Knaup. You're a German soldier, a veteran of the African campaign. Stop being so deferential."

"You are my superior."

"I'm only your Sergeant, not some officer from a Prussian military academy."

"Yes, Sergeant," Knaup said, standing a bit more upright. "But are you sure the knife was the thing that killed him? I've seen many people knifed in battle, even worse than this, and they never died. Heck, I took some shrapnel in the back just before I was taken prisoner, pretty close to where that knife is. And here I am standing next to you talking about it."

"That's more like it, Knaup," Neumann said crisply. "And you are correct that knife injuries such as this do not always result in death. However, have you noticed the smell of shit in the air?"

Knaup winced and waved his writing hand in front of his face. "Yes, it's quite unmistakable."

"Did you shit your pants when you got hit in the back with that shrapnel?"

"Of course not, Sergeant," Knaup said, insulted by the suggestion. "It hurt like hell and I screamed, but I didn't shit my pants."

"That's because injuries like that don't usually cause people to void their bowels. Some blows to the head can, if they are hard enough. And gut injuries, of course, but the most common one is strangulation. Which is why in medieval times they made women wear trousers when they were hanged."

Knaup frowned as he considered that image. "So you're saying he was strangled." He scribbled in his notebook.

"It's only a suggestion based on the smell in the air. The blood also points to another possibility."

"But he was stabbed in the back."

"And do you see any blood from that wound?"

Knaup leaned forward, squinting at the body. "Not much blood. Very astute observation, Sergeant." Another scribble.

Neumann waved the compliment away. "Obvious when one looks very closely."

Knaup bristled, but then pointed at the body with his pencil. "So there must be another wound at the front."

"Based on the blood, I'm sure if we looked we would probably find another stab wound somewhere in the captain's chest."

Neumann walked around to the side of the table, his eyes fixed on Schlipal's body. He stood at that spot for a long time, trying to commit the whole scene to memory. The noise of the kitchen was partly distracting. If this was another location, Neumann would have cleared the place out. But he knew that, despite the death of the head chef for Mess #3, life in Camp 133 had to go on. There were men that had to be fed this morning; twenty-four hundred in this mess alone, in three shifts of eight hundred. And denying these men food would create a situation worse than the murder of the chef of their mess.

Schlipal's second-in-command, a lieutenant named Frank,

stood at the entrance of the kitchen, arms folded across his chest, a cigarette hanging from his lips. He seemed more upset about the possibility of a late breakfast than he did about the death of his superior.

Of course, Neumann knew people that created dead bodies, either on their own or in large groups, didn't really care about inconveniencing others. They just killed people when and where they wanted to and left things for other people to clean up. War was similar.

Neumann motioned for Frank to step forward. The lieutenant rolled his eyes and sighed, but walked over. He said nothing, though his annoyance was palpable.

Neumann chose to ignore it. "So, you did not discover the body yourself, Lieutenant Frank?"

"I already told you I didn't." Frank grumbled around the cigarette that was still in his mouth. "It was a baker."

"And this baker, where is he?"

Frank shrugged. "I don't know. Probably back in his hut by now. Those guys come in early and are ready to leave when we come in."

"You let him go?" Corporal Knaup snapped. "A key witness to this murder and you let him go?"

The lieutenant turned to glare a Knaup. He took a pull from his cigarette and blew smoke in the corporal's direction. "It's not my duty to investigate this situation and keep witnesses here, Corporal," Frank said, reminding Knaup of the chain of command. "My job is to ensure twenty-four hundred men get their breakfast. And then their lunch and then their dinner. And with Chef Schlipal out of the picture, my job's a lot tougher now."

Sergeant Neumann raised his hand to stop Knaup from berating Frank any further. He stepped forward, not quite into the lieutenant's personal space, but since Neumann stood several inches taller, it was enough. Frank didn't step back; an officer in the Wehrmacht wouldn't step back from a lower-ranked soldier. Instead, he shifted uncomfortably on his feet and hesitated to meet Neumann's eyes.

"Terribly sorry for Corporal Knaup's outburst, Lieutenant Frank. He's only acting as my aide on a temporary basis and sometimes lacks tact when dealing with others." Neumann's voice was soft, but all three men understood the patronizing intent behind his words.

"Apologize to the Lieutenant, Corporal Knaup," Neumann said without breaking his gaze.

"That's entirely unnecessary, Sergeant Neumann," Frank said, back-pedalling from his previous comments.

"No, I insist. Corporal Knaup overstepped his boundaries and must apologize for his actions." Neumann raised his hand and waved it forward. "Corporal Knaup. Apologize."

Knaup paused for several seconds and then reluctantly offered an apology. There was no real sincerity in it yet no one seemed to care.

"See? Now we're all better," Neumann smiled at Frank, but there was no warmth in it. "So let's start this again. This baker, you said he's probably back in his hut. Which hut would that be?"

"Most of our baking staff live in Hut 4, just to the north." Frank indicated the direction with a jerk of his head. "On the main floor near the east exit. They tend to stay apart from the others because of the earliness of their hours. They want to avoid rousing the other soldiers when they wake up for their shift."

"That's quite considerate of them, don't you think, Knaup?"

"I guess," Knaup said. "I wouldn't know."

Neumann sighed, missing Aachen. He would have played along. But he put that behind him and focused on the situation. "And this young baker's name?"

"Um, uh … Beck. Private Beck."

"A baker named Beck?" Neumann asked with a chuckle. "That's very convenient."

"Apparently he comes from a long line of bakers," Frank replied.

"No doubt." Neumann said. "Okay, Lieutenant Frank. We'll get out of your way and let you get the mess ready for the first serving of breakfast. Come on, Knaup, let's go talk to this Beck fellow." Neumann moved towards the kitchen entrance.

Knaup cleared his throat loudly. Neumann stopped and turned to look at him. "Passive aggression is beneath you, Corporal Knaup. If you have a question, just ask."

"What about Captain Schlipal?" Knaup asked, pointing at the body.

Neumann shook his head with a chuckle. "Right. Thank you for reminding me, Corporal Knaup." He turned, walked over to the body, and looked at it for several seconds. "Do you have a handkerchief, Knaup? Clean or dirty, makes no difference."

The Corporal shrugged. "I'm sorry, Sergeant, I don't."

Neumann turned to Frank. "How about you, Lieutenant?"

Frank sighed, stepped into the kitchen for a moment, and returned with a steaming white towel. Neumann could see that the fingers holding the towel were red. The sergeant looked at it and the man's hand for a moment. "It's clean, if that's what you're worried about." Frank said. "We dry them in our ovens. Much faster than hanging, especially in winter.

Neumann nodded and took it. The towel was warm, almost too hot to touch, but not quite. He wrapped it around his right hand and grabbed the hilt of the knife sticking out of Schlipal's back, sliding his hand through the knuckle guard as he did so. He pulled and grunted as a pain built in his torso. He had broken a rib and cracked two others that summer, and while they had mostly mended, they still bothered Neumann if he exerted himself too much.

He placed his other hand on his injured side and pushed on his ribs while he pulled on the knife. He grunted in pain, but the bloody knife came out. A small trickle of congealed blood discharged from the wound.

Neumann wrapped the towel around the whole knife, catching his breath as he did so. He took pains not to let any part of his hands touch the weapon.

He stepped away and then held the wrapped knife out to the Corporal. Knaup and Frank both stood there, shocked at the scene that had unfolded before him. When Knaup did not move to take the knife, Neumann waved it at him, indicating he should to take it. After a moment, Knaup reluctantly accepted the knife, using only the tips of his thumb and index finger.

"Hold it more carefully than that, Knaup. I don't want you to drop it or for the towel to come unwrapped." Neumann reached out and pulled Knaup's rucksack off his shoulder. He opened the top and held it out. "Here, put it in here."

Knaup reached out for the bag. "But carefully," Neumann snapped. "I don't want it to get unwrapped."

Holding his breath, Knaup slowly lowered the knife into his rucksack. He only relaxed when he pulled his hand out. But there was a look of worry on his face.

"Okay, we're done here. Let's go." Neumann said, pushing open the door to the kitchen, intent on using the back exit to leave the building.

"But Sergeant. What about Captain Schlipal?" Lieutenant Frank called after him. "You're going to just leave him here?"

Neumann stopped and turned to smile at Frank. "Of course I am. I have a baker to interview."

"But I have 800 men coming for breakfast in less than fifteen minutes. They can't eat with a dead body in the mess."

That made Neumann laugh in earnest. "Please, Lieutenant Frank. These are German combat soldiers. I'm sure most of them have eaten next to a few dead bodies before. One more won't make a difference."

"Seriously, Sergeant Neumann. He can't stay here."

"That's not my concern. I'm not in the body disposal business."

"Neither am I. I'm only a chef in this mess."

"Apparently you're the head chef now, so you better figure it out. And whatever you do, say nothing about the knife, understand?" There was a menacing tone in Neumann's voice.

Frank nodded, saying nothing.

Neumann nodded back and gave the lieutenant a quick salute, as protocol demanded.

"Come on Knaup. Let's go."

The corporal saluted Frank, and quickly followed Neumann out of the mess.

2.

Since Beck's hut was just to the north of the mess, it was a quick walk through the cold, biting wind. Still, Neumann and Knaup tucked their chins into their chests, their hands into their pockets, and jogged the twenty-five metres to the hut directly behind Mess #3. They exchanged no words during their brief sojourn and said nothing to the group of prisoners who were clearing the drifts of snow from around the door.

There were a total of thirty-six huts in Camp 133. Every one of these two-storey, clapboard buildings were hastily constructed after the German defeat in North Africa. Since so many Germans had been taken prisoner after that Allied victory, the British government didn't think it was wise to bring them to their relatively small island, as they would only tax their already taxed resources and create havoc as prisoners made escape attempts to get across the channel and back to the Fatherland.

So the Brits turned to Canada, and the agreeable Canadians, who wanted to show that they were full partners in the war, agreed. There were already several small camps scattered across the vast Canadian landscape but larger ones were needed to handle the huge influx of captured Germans. The prairies of western Canada, more specifically, near the towns of Lethbridge and Medicine Hat, afforded such space, and had the added benefit of nearby infrastructure, such as roads and railways, to quickly transport prisoners and supplies to the camps.

The two camps, 133 near Lethbridge and 130 near Medicine Hat, were replicas of one another; each one covered what the Canadians called a "section" of land—nominally one square mile or six hundred and forty acres. The entire perimeter of the camps were surrounded by two five-metre-high fences, five metres apart, made of criss-crossed barbed wire topped with another layer of barbed wire that extend inward. Guards regularly patrolled the space between these two high fences, sometimes with dogs.

Spaced out along the fence were twenty-two towers, each one manned by at least four armed guards with shoot-to-kill orders. Twenty metres inside the main perimeter was another barbed-wire fence, one metre high. This twenty metres was a no man's land where no prisoner was allowed to venture. Guards also had a shoot-to-kill orders if any prisoner entered this area, but usually gave shouted warnings.

The double-gated entrance in the middle of the southern border of the camp was the only way in or out. There was a building just inside that entrance that acted as a detention area for prisoners who had violated some camp rule or needed to be separated from the overall population for their own safety. About one hundred metres north of the gate were the barracks or "huts," as some prisoners called them. Thirty-six two-storey buildings were arranged in six rows of six, running north and south, with a large mess in the middle of each row.

Further north of the barracks were fifteen more buildings, arranged in a pattern of two smaller buildings around another larger one at the end of each row of barracks. These buildings acted a classrooms, workshops, and administration buildings used by the prisoners. The Germans had plenty of opportunity and free time to take a wide variety of classes, work on hobbies, sports, or reacquaint themselves with trades they had put aside to fight in the war. The camp had facilities and equipment for almost every trade, everything from carpentry to glassblowing.

Further north of these buildings were three even larger structures. The smallest of the three was the medical building where prisoners were treated for injuries or any sicknesses they developed while in the camp. It sat centred between the other two large buildings, which were actually the largest structures of their kind in western Canada. These were the recreational halls for the camp; large open-space buildings used for performances, gatherings, or special events. Each one of these buildings could hold up to 5,000 prisoners at a time.

And because all of this was built in the middle of the southern Alberta prairie, it was exposed to the constant wind which buffeted the area. Although the huts acted to buffer these winds in the camp, they also caused the snow to swirl between the buildings, resulting in large drifts along the sides of the buildings and the doors.

For the past few days, it was almost a full time job for a crew of prisoners to prevent the snow from rising past the windows, as well as to maintain the framework of paths that ran through the camps between the many buildings like a giant grid. Fortunately for those shovelling and sweeping, the Canadian snow was light, not the heavy, wet snow that fell in Germany. And as prisoners took more direct routes between buildings, there was another compliment of informal paths that snaked through the camp.

Arriving at the barracks in the third row, just north of the mess, Neumann nodded in greeting to a prisoner who opened the door for them at the entrance of the hut. Inside, Knaup and Neumann stamped their boots to clear the snow. Neumann rubbed the cold from his face and Knaup gave a quick shiver.

"I know what you're going to say, Knaup, but please don't ask me about the knife." Neumann said as he stood by the door, waiting for his eyes to adjust to the light inside the hut. "And say nothing about it to this Beck fellow."

"Of course, Sergeant. Whatever you say. But I wasn't going to say anything about the knife."

"No? So you aren't curious at all?"

"Of course I'm curious," Knaup said, crossing his arms to

rub the cold from his shoulders and forearms. "I've never seen anyone remove a knife from a murder victim the way you did."

"So you've seen that done before? Seen someone remove a knife from a body before?"

"Well yes, Sergeant. In battle it happened every day. But that's not murder, that's war. Not counting that, Captain Schlipal is only the second murder victim I've seen in my entire life."

"The second? You mean you've seen another?"

Knaup looked at Neumann to see if the man was joking. When he realized that he wasn't, he spoke. "Have you forgotten Captain Mueller already? Remember this past summer you asked me to find Doctor Kleinjeld and take him to the classroom without telling me that poor Captain Mueller was hanged in the corner? That was quite a shock for me."

"Right. Mueller." Neumann winced, remembering his rib injuries that resulted from that situation. His bones may have started to heal, but the arrival of winter had created an ache in his chest that he knew would stay with him for the rest of his life. And not just because of the effect cold weather would have on his weakened body. He doubted he would ever shake the disillusionment from discovering who had killed Mueller. And the disappointment as to why. It was a stupid reason to kill a man, a senseless waste of life. Of two lives, in the end.

But they were living in a time of war. Neumann's second war in fact, so there was plenty of wasteful killing. What was one dead soldier when millions were dying? Well, now two considering what had happened to Chef Schlipal. Three if you counted Mueller's murderer.

Neumann sighed but not too deeply because of his protesting ribs. "I'm sorry, Knaup. I'm used to dealing with Corporal Aachen always questioning my actions. Wondering why I'm doing something. I have to remind myself that you're not Aachen."

Knaup smiled at that statement. "As I said, I am curious about why you removed the knife from Captain Schlipal's body, but I figured you had your reasons and if you wished to share those reasons with me, you would."

"I will Knaup, don't you worry about that. But as of this moment, let's just not say anything about it to Private Beck when we interview him. In fact, please don't say anything about the knife to anyone. Your job at the moment is to look intimidating."

"That's a little difficult for me, Sergeant. I'm not as imposing as you and Corporal Aachen."

Neumann turned and poked Knaup in the chest. "You're a German soldier, are you not?" he hissed in a sharp whisper. "You served with honour for your country in Africa, one of the bloodiest campaigns in the history of mankind. You have killed many enemy soldiers, Knaup, not just with your rifle, but close up, with your hands."

Knaup blinked quickly, his face turning red.

"I've seen your record, Knaup. When you asked me if you could help, I had to see what kind of soldier you were. You may be a quiet, shy fellow at times, but I know what you've done on the battlefield. And I know that when you attacked that machine gun nest just before the Fall of Tobruk, you killed those three Tommies, one with your knife and the other with your bare hands. And they didn't see some quiet lad from Dresden. They saw a man who came to kill them."

Neumann saw the faraway look in the young corporal's eyes as he relived those desperate moments in which he had to kill or be killed. Knaup's face hardened at the memory. Neumann gave him a sharp punch to the shoulder to bring him back to the present.

"That's it, Knaup. That's the look I want to see. The look of a strong and terrifying German soldier who's seen enough combat to last a lifetime."

Knaup looked at the sergeant. The tension in his body had lessened once he realized he was no longer on the battlefield. But the hardness in his face remained. And even Neumann, who had faced war and battle and death in two world wars, was a bit afraid of him.

"Okay," Neumann said. "Let's go find this baker."

3.

As they walked into the hut's southeast corner on the first floor, it was obvious that the bakers had purposely congregated in this area, just as Neumann had been told. There was a layer of white dust everywhere, and the smell of flour and sugar and butter hung in the air, mingling with the scent of sweat and the musk of men living in close quarters. That musky scent, along with the staleness of lingering cigarette smoke, permeated every single building, even when they were empty during a count. There was no escaping the smell of over 12,000 German prisoners of war jammed together in a square mile camp at the edge of a seemingly insignificant town in the middle of the Canadian prairie.

It also seemed that everyone in this section of hut was in their bunks, sleeping. Most of the sleepers wore their kitchen whites after a long night of baking for the 2,400 men in their mess, some of them still with spots of flour and unbaked pastry clinging to their smocks.

Neumann scanned the area and wondered if any of the other huts had a dedicated space for their bakers.

Based on his dealings connected to Captain Mueller's death this past summer, he knew the legionnaires, German soldiers who had served in the French Foreign Legion before and during the early parts of the war, had their own hut in the camp. Many others were loosely decamped based on what battalion or division they were part of, which part of the forces they had served under—the Heer, Luftwaffe, or Kriegsmarine—and further based on which division or battalion they had been divided in. So Neumann pondered if any of the other prisoners who worked in similar trades—cooks, teachers, doctors, administrators, farm workers, etc., or those who had come from similar parts of Germany—had made similar arrangements; if they had created small neighbourhoods in other areas of the camp the way various people had done in his village before for the war, like neighbourhoods for tradesmen, the rich, the poor, and the Jews.

Neumann inwardly chastised himself for not thinking about such a thing before. He told himself that once he had dealt with the Schlipal situation, he would determine if such neighbourhoods did exist. As the head of Civil Security of Camp 133, he had easy access to prisoner information and mapping these communities could help him predict future conflicts.

His thoughts wandered to his hometown. He tried to

envision which neighbourhoods survived the war and how much of its social, political, and economic structure had endured. He realized that there was one part of the town, the Jewish district, which would never be the same. That he would never again shop for books at Ismer's, never buy meats and cheese at Phillip's and Nephew while he listened to the old man constantly complaining about his neighbours, and never discuss music with Bachenheimer while lingering at his shop on the corner across from the synagogue.

A deep sadness came over Neumann as he thought about the destruction of this part of his town. Not just about the destruction, but why and how little he could have done to stop it. Not only was he helpless to prevent it, but even if he had still been heading up the village police department instead of training young soldiers how not to get killed in battle, he would have been called on to play a major role in removing his longtime neighbours from their homes and businesses.

The fact that he had been spared this duty did not lessen the guilt he felt or change how hollow his town would feel with one of its key group of citizens removed. There were many in his town who would have celebrated the removal of the Jews, who would have jeered at their longtime neighbours as they were moved out into some ghetto in Poland. But even they would begin to realize that something important had been taken away from them and that the community, and the country as a whole, would be tarnished by this. No matter how the war turned out, there was no way Germany would escape the stain and guilt of what they had done to many of their fellow countrymen who practiced a different faith.

Neumann was brought back to the present by Corporal Knaup gently tapping him on the shoulder. "Sergeant?" he asked quietly. "Are you okay?"

"Oh yes, Knaup," Neumann said with a slight shake of his head. "This baking smell reminded me of home and I took to reminiscing about the old town."

Knaup smiled, looking like a student who has just realized that the teacher he had long feared was a human being with normal thoughts, dreams, and desires. "Of course, Sergeant. I do that all the time. Thinking about my mother, my father, and my two sisters. They haven't experienced any of the bombing that some other parts of the country have, so I'm pleased they are still doing relatively well."

"Yes, I've heard that Dresden has been spared from much of the war when compared to other cities."

Knaup's smiled widened. "We're very lucky that we are of little strategic significance and should make it through the war without a scratch."

"I hope so, for your family's sake."

Knaup looked off for a moment and then turned to Neumann. "Do you have family, Sergeant?"

"I have a sister in Frankfurt," he replied. "Some nieces and nephews but we haven't talked in years so I have no idea how they're doing."

"My father has a cousin he doesn't talk to anymore. They were close as youths but now …" Knaup trailed off, then sighed.

After a moment, he gave Neumann a pleading look. "I'm sorry if this seems out of place, Sergeant, but do you have any idea when we'll be going home?"

Neumann offered a sigh of his own and shook his head. Knaup looked a bit dejected by this response. "In my experience, it's best not to think about such things, Corporal," Neumann said softly.

"It's just that I've been hearing stories about the situation back home. That with the Allies pushing so fast through France and Belgium that if we don't respond, things will end very quickly."

Since the invasion of central Europe in June, everyone in the camp was quite aware of the situation. The Canadians had been trumpeting every single one of the Allies' successes, no matter how big or small, since D-Day, trying to convince the prisoners that their war was over and they should adopt the tenants of democracy, whatever that meant. Of course, the camp population had their own means of getting news from the outside world; through coded messages in letters from family and friends back home. And from their secret network of shortwave radios that various prisoners had illegally built out of various camp supplies. With a population of 12,000 from almost every single part of the German armed forces, there were plenty of prisoners with the technical and scientific skills to build a radio.

Even so, the news from these sources wasn't good either. The Allies had made huge progress since the invasion, eliminating all the gains in Western Europe that Germany had fought hard for in the early parts of the war, pushing back almost to the border. And even though the Russians had stopped their push on the Eastern Front, everyone suspected that Stalin was just in a holding pattern, replenishing his troops and improving the stretched Soviet supply network. It was only a matter of time before the Ivans made a push for Berlin.

"But there is also talk of the Führer pulling back to lull the Allies into a false sense of security and then striking back hard when they are least expecting it," Knaup said with more enthusiasm. "Which would be a wonderful thing even though it would delay us getting home."

Neumann cleared his head of thoughts of home and a German victory. He rubbed his hands together quickly. "War has its own schedule and no matter what we think, hear, or wish, it will do what it pleases on its own time," he said with bite in his voice. "And since I've been a soldier for two of them, I've learned it's best to forget those kinds of thoughts and focus on doing your duty when you can. That's the only way to make it without getting killed or going crazy."

"Yes Sergeant. That's quite wise," Knaup said. "Shall I go looking for Private Beck, then? Or would you prefer to search for him?" Neumann gestured for Knaup to go ahead and the corporal stepped forward, clapping his hands several times to get the attention of the sleeping bakers.

"Attention! Attention all of you! We are looking for Private Beck," Knaup shouted. He banged on a couple of bunks. "Private Beck, you are being summoned!"

There were groans of complaint and a few shouted rude

comments. A baker from one of the top bunks Knaup had hit threw something that looked like a rock. The corporal easily dodged it and the object bounced softly across the floor and rolled to a stop against the wall where Neumann was standing. The sergeant looked down and saw it was some type of baked roll. He bent down, picked it up, and squeezed it gently in his hand. It was soft and smelled fresh. Neumann dusted the roll off and took a small bite. He smiled at the salty yet sweet taste and took another bite.

By now, Knaup had turned on the baker who had thrown the bun, banging his fist on the side of the bunk again. "You! What is your name?" Knaup shouted, shaking the bunk. "Tell me your name!"

The baker wasn't intimidated by this shouting. He told Knaup to fuck off, then pulled his blanket over his head and rolled over. The corporal responded by grabbing the blanket and tossing it to the floor. The baker sat up and whirled around quickly, fists raised. It was difficult to see how big the soldier was, but his fists were large, scarred on the knuckles, and he had several tattoos on his arms suggesting he was some type of naval regular. "Who the fuck do you think you are?" the baker shouted back, preparing to swing himself off the bunk to face off with Knaup.

Knaup shoved the baker back onto the bunk, holding him down by pressing one hand against his chest. The baker took a couple of swings at Knaup but they were batted away by Knaup's other hand. Neumann watched passively, chewing on the roll. He smiled slightly when Knaup started slapping the baker across the face. The baker struggled for a few moments, but the fight quickly went out of him. Any other prisoners who had groaned and complained at the interruption of their sleep were doing their best to stay out of the situation.

"What the fuck do you want?" the baker hissed at Knaup. "I did nothing."

"You threw an object at the head of Civil Security. That can get you put on report."

"Jesus, it was only a bread roll," the baker said. "How the fuck was I to know it was you assholes when you just come in here shouting your head off, waking everyone up."

Knaup started a retort to the baker's response but Neumann interrupted him. "Ask him about Private Beck?"

Knaup looked at the sergeant, nodded, and then turned the baker who was lying on his bunk with his arms raised in appeasement. "Which one is Private Beck's bunk?" Knaup demanded.

"Over there," the pinned baker said with a jerk of his head. "Three bunks over. On the bottom. Underneath Pletcher."

Knaup released the baker with a shove and bent down to look through the other bunks to find Beck. The lower half of the third bunk was empty. "He's not there, Sergeant," Knaup answered.

The prisoner above the empty bunk, Pletcher, was sitting up. He was skinny and still wearing his kitchen whites. "He went to clean up," he shouted to Neumann across the room, and pointed towards the showers near the centre of the building. Knaup stared hard at him.

"Honest. That's what he said he was going to do," Pletcher said. "Take a shower. 'Wash the shit of the day off' he said."

Knaup nodded once and then turned to Sergeant Neumann. "Beck's in the shower, Sergeant."

Neumann nodded. "I heard. Good work, Knaup. Let's go."

As the two of them walked away. The bakers grumbled, responding with rude gestures behind their backs. More bread was harmlessly tossed in their direction. Knaup and Neumann ignored the taunts but the sergeant did bend over to pick up a few of the rolls. He put those in his jacket pocket.

4.

They found Beck coming out of the shower, naked, dripping with water and drying his head with his towel. He was older than Knaup, in his late twenties. Neumann figured he had probably been stocky while he was in a combat unit, but after months in the camp with generous amounts of food provided by the Canadians, he had gained plenty of weight. His chest sagged and his belly hung low with rolls of fat. After drying his hair, Beck started on his skin, most of his body covered with a fine layer of hair.

He was several steps out of the showering area before he saw Neumann and Knaup waiting for him. "Shit," he whispered, shaking his head. But he moved forward, still naked, to greet them and offered a meaty hand to the sergeant.

"Private Beck," Neumann said, accepting the handshake. He looked Beck in the eye, attempting to discern if this baker had anything to do with death of Chef Schlipal. "My name is—"

"I know who you are," Beck said in a clear baritone.

Beck's grip was firm but not overly powerful. So he wasn't interested in a game of bravado to prove he was stronger than Neumann. He gave a quick glance over to the silent and now stolid Corporal Knaup, yet only nodded in greeting, the way a private would normally greet a corporal—nothing more. There was no look of fear or deceit in his eyes, just a tired expression of resignation.

"I was hoping I'd have a little more time before you'd find me," he said. "Which is why I took a shower."

"Sorry Private, death waits for no one, especially when someone's been murdered," Neumann said. He switched to a conciliatory tone. "We can talk while you dress, if it makes you more comfortable."

Beck tilted his head to the side and, without a word, turned away from Neumann and Knaup and headed towards a series of hooks along the wall, upon which hung various pieces of clothing. Since it was close to breakfast, there were only a few men in the showering area. Most of them dressed or left the area as quickly as possible once they realized Sergeant Neumann was there to talk someone. A couple of prisoners who walked in, making jokes about a card game a night before, hastily turned around and left once they spotted the sergeant.

In less than twenty seconds, there was no one left in the showering area, save for Neumann, Knaup, and Beck. Beck chuckled at this as he pulled on his boxers, shoving his bulbous penis into the shorts. "You can sure clear out a place, Sergeant," Beck said as he shifted his hips to get his genitals into a comfortable position. He reached around to grab an undershirt from the hook.

"They've probably all heard about Schlipal being dead and about you discovering his body," Neumann said with a shrug.

"Already? I found him barely an hour ago."

"It's a small camp," Neumann said as Beck pulled his shirt over his large belly. "So, how did you find him?"

Beck adjusted his shirt, pulling the material away from the few wet spots in his body. "I just walked into the mess area and there he was."

"Dead?"

"Definitely dead. That knife in his back was a good sign of that."

Behind him, Neumann could hear Knaup scribbling in his notebook. Beck looked over at the corporal for several seconds, then turned his attention back to Neumann.

"You sure he was dead?"

"No disrespect, Sergeant Neumann, but I've seen plenty of dead bodies in the past five years, so when I say he was dead, he was dead." Beck bent over to pull on his pants.

Neumann looked down at the private for several seconds. Beck pulled his pants over his boxers before doing up the button. He looked up to see Neumann still staring at him.

"Come on, Private. If you want us to finish this quickly you have to tell me the complete truth. If you don't, then I'll have to assume you're involved somehow."

Beck's eyes narrowed and he grimaced, like an adolescent being falsely accused of some minor infraction. He glanced at Knaup, searching for support from another junior-ranked soldier yet got nothing in return. The baker rolled his eyes and shook his head. "Fine, I called out his name a couple of times and then stepped up to his table to get a better look."

"Did you touch him?"

Beck shook his head.

"Are you sure?"

"Very sure. My hands were covered in flour and I didn't think it was wise to get it all over him." Knaup scribbled this comment in his book. Again, Beck glanced over but only for a second.

"Were you surprised?"

"Surprised? Of course I was surprised."

"Surprised by the fact Chef Schlipal was dead or that someone had killed him?"

Beck seemed confused by the question. After a moment he said. "I'm not sure why you're interrogating me here, Sergeant. I'm trying to help."

Neumann smiled a friendly smile. "Sorry Private, we aren't even close to an interrogation here; I'm just asking questions. And the answers help me find out other things, like maybe why someone wanted to kill Chef Schlipal, especially coming from people like you who worked closely with him. But you're right. You are trying to help, so I'll ask the question again but in two parts. First, were you surprised to find Captain Schlipal dead?"

Beck gave Neumann an incredulous look. "Of course I was

surprised to find him dead! Sure there's the war, but we're in the middle of a fucking prisoner camp thousands of miles from any sort of front, so you don't expect to find dead bodies all over the place. Especially in the middle of the mess where everyone eats."

"Good answer, Private Beck. Very good. Now the second part of the question—"

Beck cut him off, "Are you asking me if I had any reason to kill him?"

Neumann shrugged and raised an eyebrow. "You? Or anyone else you may know. How about it, Private Beck? Any ideas?"

Beck stepped back, raised his hands, and shook his head. "I have no idea. Really, I don't."

"So everyone in the mess liked Captain Schlipal? Everyone thought he was a good head chef and had no problems with him? He was easy to work for, treated everyone fairly and with respect?" There was a sarcastic tone to Neumann's voice.

"No, Schlipal was a total asshole," Beck replied. "Always yelling at someone, always calling someone a cocksucker or a motherfucker, complaining about how we made the bread, complaining about it being too salty one day, too sweet the next, too dry, too moist, all kinds of shit like that. And we were just the bakers. He was worse to his cooks."

"So he was a harsh taskmaster. And as you said, a total asshole, abusive to his underlings," Neumann turned to Knaup. "Make sure you get that down accurately, Corporal." Knaup nodded and scribbled in his notebook.

Beck frowned. "Yeah, but that's nothing really new in the kitchen business. Most executive chefs are assholes. They're always yelling at everyone for whatever reason and Schlipal was no different. It's a tough job running the kitchen, especially here where he's got to feed 2,400 hungry Germans three times a day. Not something I'd like to do. I'm just happy with baking my bread and the odd bit of dessert here and there."

"Okay, being an asshole is part of his job," Neumann said. "That's something with which I'm quite familiar, as Corporals Knaup and Aachen could tell you. Although they won't say it to my face. And I can tell from the look on your face that you're thinking the same thing." Neumann stepped forward and placed an arm around Beck's wide shoulders. The baker seemed surprised by this gesture, stiffening slightly, but didn't move away. Neumann slowly turned Beck around so they faced the wall. He leaned close to the baker.

"So Private Beck, one more question, if you don't mind," Neumann whispered. He did not wait for a response. "A few months ago I approached Captain Schlipal about Command's concern about pilfering in Mess #3." Beck stiffened and tried to pull away but Neumann held him in place. "That it was much too high for a mess of his size. Sure, we expect some, but not as much as what was going on there. He told me to fuck off and, as you might expect, I became a bit of an asshole. A lot worse than I am today. A lot worse. Today is nothing compared to the kind of asshole I can become, you can count on that. So there was pilfering taking place, and I haven't checked the numbers in a couple of months. So my last question to you,

Private Beck, is if I did check today, would I discover that the pilfering from Mess #3 has gone up again past normal levels?"

Beck's face turned white and his cocky attitude disappeared. Neumann saw fear on Beck's face, though he wasn't sure if it was because Beck was afraid of him. Or something else. Or both.

"I'm only a b-b-baker," Beck stuttered. "I bake bread, every day—that's all I do. Bake bread."

"And the odd dessert, here and there," Neumann added.

"I don't get involved in that kind of stuff. I'm just a private who bakes bread."

"But you probably hear things. As I said, it's a small camp. Big in many respects, but small in many others. People hear things, don't they, Private? Just like everyone has probably heard that Captain Schlipal is dead and you found the body."

Beck looked at the sergeant for several seconds and swallowed hard. "I didn't kill him," he finally said. "I didn't kill Captain Schlipal."

"Of course you didn't. You already told me that and I believe you. You're only a baker who bakes bread every day with the odd dessert now and then. But even bakers like you hear things, see things. Am I right?"

Beck nodded, blinking in fear.

"And though you don't get involved in such things, which is commendable—don't forget to note that down, Corporal Knaup; we want Private Beck to know we aren't accusing him of any crimes ..." Knaup scribbled and Neumann continued,

"I believe you and anyone else working in the kitchen would notice if there was pilfering going on."

Beck looked at Neumann, then at Knaup, then at Neumann again. He nodded.

"Very good, Private. And please don't worry that you didn't report it; I understand it's hard to know where to stand on such matters when you don't want to seem like an informer. But I'm going to need you to tell me if you did notice an increase in pilfering since I talked to Captain Schlipal in June, since it might have played a role in his death. Do you understand?"

Beck gave a stiff nod.

"And your answer? Do you believe the pilfering has increased to previous levels?" Neumann asked, cocking his head.

After several seconds, the baker reluctantly nodded.

Neumann released Beck instantly and backed away. The baker stumbled at the sudden movement and had to place his hand against the wall to keep his balance.

"Excellent," Neumann said, clapping his hands once. "There's a good chance I'll be back to ask some more questions. But for now, thank you for your help, Private Beck."

Neumann turned and quickly headed for the door. Knaup gave Beck a look, one mixed with pity and apology, but then followed right behind the sergeant.

5.

Just before they stepped outside the hut into the cold December air, Neumann and Knaup stopped to allow a large group of prisoners to leave so they could make it to their round of breakfast. Each of the camp's six messes had to serve 2,400 prisoners a meal three times a day. But each mess only sat 800. So each meal was further divided into three sittings. It was a few minutes before the second sitting and the hut's double doors were held open as large numbers of prisoners headed over to eat. Cold air and drifts of snow blew in and Neumann pulled Knaup aside so they could stand a few metres away from the chill and the prisoners.

Their presence did not go unnoticed. The men glanced over at them with concern. Some probably were aware of the situation with Chef Schlipal, while others were wondering why the head of Civil Security was there. Every so often a prisoner would nod or verbalize a greeting to the sergeant. For the most part, the prisoners gave them a wide berth.

"What's next in our plan, Sergeant?" Knaup asked, speaking slightly louder so he could be heard above the noise of wind blowing through the open door and the sound of many soldiers heading out for breakfast.

"At the moment, I think it's wise if you head over to the hospital and see if Chef Schlipal's body has arrived."

Knaup's face fell with disappointment so Neumann slapped him hard on the shoulder. "Stop being a baby, Corporal Knaup," Neumann snapped. "You did well with the baker in the bunk and with Beck, but if you keep sulking like a child when I order you to do something you don't like, then I'll just find someone else to assist me. Do you understand me, Corporal?"

Knaup snapped to attention in response to the sergeant's tone. His face, though, turned red with embarrassment.

"You asked to become involved in the civil security of this camp and since Corporal Aachen is still feeling the effects of his injuries, I decided to take you on," Neumann continued. Several prisoners passing by chuckled at the scene, but an angry look from Neumann sent them hurrying away. Neumann turned back to Knaup. "So, what did I just order you to do?"

"To go to the hospital and see if Chef Schlipal's body has arrived."

"So what will you do?"

"As you ordered, Sergeant."

Neumann slapped Knaup on the shoulder again, but not as a hard as before. "Good," he said in a more relaxed voice. "You never served with me in combat, Knaup, so you don't know that I can be quite informal with my subordinates. But remember that when I ask you to do something, even in an offhand kind of way, I'm still a sergeant giving you an order in a time of war, so I expect you to follow those orders no matter how informal or insignificant they may seem."

Knaup nodded. Neumann slapped him again. "Okay, get going to the hospital."

Knaup clicked his heels and quickly turned to head out the door. A few steps away, he stopped and turned back. He hesitated for a second but then asked, "and what shall I do there, Sergeant?"

"Whatever anyone there asks you to do, except leave the body. I want you present during any examination by Dr. Kleinjeld or whoever else. And I want you to take as detailed notes as you can, even more detailed than the ones you take for me. I want you to document everything anyone says or does. Everything."

"Yes, Sergeant." Knaup said with a nod. "I will endeavour to take excellent notes."

"And don't let anyone tell you to leave so they can work on the body on their own. Or because of some kind of medical excuse. Even if they order you to do so, even if they are an officer, tell them that Sergeant Neumann has ordered you to stay. And my commands as head of Civil Security supersede others in this camp."

Again, Knaup nodded. Neumann walked up to him and whispered, "And nothing about what you have in your rucksack, yes Knaup?"

"Yes, Sergeant." The corporal turned and left the hut.

Instead of leaving by the same south doors, Neumann went the other way, traversing the hut, moving through the rows of two-men bunks to the western side of the building.

There were a few men heading this way too, and most of them hurried to get out of Neumann's way. He stopped just inside the northwest doors to turn the collar of his winter coat up and pull his knitted cap over his ears.

Another prisoner suddenly appeared at his side. "Wishing you were back in Africa, eh August?"

Neumann turned to the voice and a grin spread across his face. "Captain Liszt," Neumann said, giving a quick but casual salute. Liszt paused, shook his head, and saluted back. Liszt had been a platoon commander in Africa, but now served as a music teacher and conductor for the Philharmonic Orchestra of Camp 133. Made up of various members of varying talent from the camp, the orchestra was a haphazard affair by Liszt's standards, but was probably the best orchestra in this part of the world. Some of its members had been world-class musicians prior to the war, including Liszt himself who was also one of the best musical conductors in Germany.

Like many veterans of the First World War, he volunteered for the German army in the late 1930s and was accepted back in. Many of these soldiers, especially those with combat experience, had been offered a commission as an officer. Neumann was one of the few who rejected this offer, preferring to serve in the regular ranks as a non-comm.

"How are the preparations for the Christmas concert coming along?" Neumann asked.

Liszt rolled his eyes and shook his head. "Musicians. They are never ready."

Neumann laughed. "I always thought the conductor was usually too much of a perfectionist, expecting us to get everything just right during rehearsal when he knew we would always deliver when it came time to perform."

Liszt was about to offer a retort, but Neumann continued, "Besides, there's a reason it's called 'rehearsal,' so you can prepare and repeat and make mistakes and then know where those mistakes are and fix them. For me, my best performances were always whenever I had the most terrible rehearsals the night before. The conductor would yell at us, call us names, rant and rave. But after our performance he'd be full of praise for our efforts. Of course, that's because conductors usually think it's because of them that the musicians pulled together, but they are only partly right. It's like going into battle; the commander can give directions and orders, but in the end, if the men and equipment on the ground don't work together, then all will be lost."

Liszt stepped in front of Neumann and tapped the sergeant's chest. "This is why you should be part of my orchestra, August."

"I haven't played in years. I don't think I could be up to your standards."

"Bah, it wouldn't take you that long. A bit of yelling and prodding from the conductor and you'd be in top form again," Liszt said with a grin. "At least in top form for you, which would be suitable for this orchestra."

"You're very encouraging."

"That's why I need someone like you in my orchestra. Not just for your musicianship. Listen August, I was a decent commander in Africa, but only adequate. I'm the same as a conductor. You, however, are a true leader of men. You actually inspire them rather than just lead them. And I need you in my orchestra, especially since we're going to be performing outside the camp."

"You're going outside?" Neumann said, surprised.

"Our Canadian neighbours, the fine people of the city of Lethbridge, heard about our orchestra, and requested a performance in town since they are forbidden to enter the camp," Liszt said. "It's a chance for us to show them that we aren't just the enemy, that we are humane people with skill, history, and culture. Which is why I need someone like you, someone who can lead from the pit, to inspire all my musicians to reach their potential even if they are just a corporal from Düsseldorf who happens to play music on the side."

"I gave up music years ago when I became a soldier." Neumann paused, then added, "Again."

"But there is no need for you to be a soldier anymore," Liszt said, flicking the pocket of Neumann's winter coat. "There is no need for you to wear a uniform underneath this anymore."

The majority of the prisoners in the camp wore the required uniform of a prisoner of war: a blue cloth shirt, with a large red circle on the back, and trousers. The official reason for the circle was that if a prisoner escaped, he would be easy to spot in the wilderness because of it. And if they tried to remove the circle in an effort to blend in to a crowd, it would be next to impossible to do so with a giant hole in the back of their shirt.

But everyone, from the prisoners to the Veterans Guards who guarded them, knew the red circle was something the Canadians could use as a target to shoot an escaping prisoner.

Neumann and many prisoners who still served in some kind of official administrative capacity for the camp, or had some kind of special dispensation, were allowed to wear the uniforms of whatever group they had served under in the German forces, save for those who served in the SS or Gestapo. Those uniforms and any other National Socialism symbols were forbidden. But Neumann could wear his regular Wehrmacht uniform.

"I have my duty," Neumann said, defending his choice of wardrobe. "So I dress like someone who does."

"Duty? Duty to who?" Liszt asked, with distaste in his voice.

"Duty to the men of this camp," Neumann said, after a moment of thought. "No matter who I answer to in the command structure of this camp, that's who I serve. The men of this camp. It's my job to ensure their safety while they're here."

"What about Schlipal?"

"You heard about Schlipal?"

"Everyone's heard about Schlipal," Liszt said with a tilt of his head. "So, do you have a duty to him?"

"Schlipal was a member of this camp so I have a duty to find out what happened to him."

"The same way you had a duty to find out what happened to Captain Meuller?"

"Of course."

"But at what cost? Both you and Corporal Aachen suffered serious injuries because of that. Now you have Corporal Knaup joining your crew."

"Knaup is a good man."

"Which is why you shouldn't put him in harm's way."

Neumann laughed. "I'm not putting him in harm's way. He asked me if he could help so he could learn more about policing as a possible trade for his life back in Dresden after the war. And I said yes."

"You could have said no."

"Why would I do that? Aachen and I needed help."

"Because it can be a dangerous job."

"Knaup is a soldier in the Wehrmacht. That's a dangerous job."

"But that danger passed when we were all captured. There is no need to go looking for it again."

"He wanted to help and there was no way I could deny him from helping us to carry out our duty to the camp."

"You and your … duty."

"Duty is the reason why I volunteered to be a soldier again even though I spent two years of hell in the Great War. I didn't sign up again because I was just inspired by the words of our Führer and of the other leaders of our country. I signed up to fight and serve because Germany was at war and as a German it was my duty to do so. You were the same, Liszt. You could have stayed home, found some kind of administrative job or even a performance position in one of the military orchestras. But you chose to serve on the front lines."

"But that was war. And that part is over for us. I see no reason to put my life on the line again."

"That's because your duty is different now. It's to your music and the orchestra which is used to entertain us. So in many ways, your duty is the same as mine, to the men of the camp. To make their lives here more bearable."

Liszt smiled at Neumann and wagged a finger at him. "This is why I need someone like you in my orchestra, Sergeant Neumann."

"I appreciate the invitation, but I just don't have the time. Especially with this Schlipal situation."

"Be careful with that."

Neumann only nodded. The two men stood silently at the door. A burst of cold hit them as three prisoners entered the hut, and Neumann and Liszt winced.

"I hate this weather," Neumann said. "I really hate it here. It is a cold, desolate place. No wonder the Canadians are tough bastards on the battlefield if they come from a place like this."

"I don't miss North Africa, either," Liszt said. He saluted Neumann, gave him a quick wink, and walked out into the cold.

6.

Steeling himself, Neumann stepped out into the Canadian winter. He didn't mind the idea of winter; his village got lots of snow during those cold months and temperatures did drop past freezing for several weeks. At home, the humidity in the air also allowed the cold to seep deeply into one's bones, no matter how warmly you dressed.

But the cold here was dry and sharp, with a relentless wind. It made the air feel much colder than it actually was, and brought frostbite much faster than expected. And the snow that this land created, more like sand than the soft, fluffy snow of home, blew around like pieces of glass.

What made it worse were Neumann's injuries from the summer. Because the cold and the wind caused him to tense up and breathe in short gasps, it only exacerbated the pain in his recently healed ribs. The pain then made him catch his breath which, in turn, created more pain. It was a vicious cycle. So by the time Neumann made it to his hut, he was completely annoyed and angry at the pain he was experiencing.

He stood inside the door for a few minutes to compose himself. Two soldiers ambled over to see if he needed help but he waved them away. They hovered nearby. As the head of Civil Security, he could not afford to look weak. His reputation as a tough son of a bitch was at risk. He gathered all his strength, stood up straight, and gave the two men a smile and a wave. "Damn Canadian ice. Took a tumble into a snowdrift," he said, faking a sheepish smile.

The prisoners chuckled at his feigned predicament and saluted him, moving away. Neumann walked in the opposite direction in between rows of bunks.

When he arrived at his bunk, he slowly sat down on the mattress, letting out a long sigh of relief. His ribs still hurt, but not as much as before. He contemplated laying his head on his pillow, but knew if he did, he wouldn't get up for several hours. Instead, he reached under his pillow for one of the tiny boxes Dr. Kleinjeld had given him. Inside the box was a morphine syrette, a small, soft metal tube about half the size of his thumb with a small needle on the end covered by a plastic seal. The morphine could be administered by breaking the plastic seal, jabbing the needle anywhere into the skin, and squeezing the tube. Kleinjeld had given Neumann morphine while he was in hospital and had prescribed him a few vials after he was discharged in case the pain in his ribs got too bad.

Neumann looked at the syrette. He knew it would make

him feel good for a little while, but then he would want another one. In his village, he had seen some of the effects of morphine and other similar drugs on certain people, and it wasn't good.

Neumann stared hard at the syrette. He recalled how it felt when Dr. Kleinjeld administered it to him while he was in hospital, thought of how the morphine took away the pain and replaced it with a sense of calm euphoria. Just that memory seemed to lessen the pain. He tucked the box under his pillow and sighed with relief.

"Who's dead?" asked a voice from above. It was Corporal Klaus Aachen, Neumann's regular assistant. Like Knaup, Aachen was young—in his early 20s—but had seen plenty of combat. He was short, stocky, but had lost some weight due to injuries he had suffered during the summer—which is why Neumann took Knaup on as another assistant. Aachen lay on his back reading a Karl May novel.

"Schlipal," Neumann replied.

Aachen sat up quickly in surprise, wincing in pain as he did so. "That's not good."

"No, it's not," Neumann said without looking up. "Not good at all."

"You remember that conversation we had with Schlipal about pilfering this past summer?" Aachen asked

"Clearly. That's one of the first things I thought about when I saw his body."

"We're going to have to check to see if that played a role in his death."

"Again, another thought that came to mind when I saw his

body." Neumann said. "I might have to talk to that asshole Sergeant Heidfeld and his minions."

Aachen swung his legs over and lowered himself from the top bunk to the floor, his face tightened with pain. He sat on the lower bunk across from Neumann's. "I may not be myself yet, but I will come with you, Sergeant Neumann. You'll have nothing to fear from them."

Neumann laughed. "The only thing I fear about Heidfeld and his goons is how much my split knuckles will hurt after I knock them to the floor."

"I will join you and we will share in that pain," Aachen said with a laugh. "And Knaup can join us too, if he's up for it."

"Knaup is definitely up for it," Neumann said. He told Aachen how Knaup had handled the baker in the bunk and the information from Private Beck.

"You're quite sure this Beck has nothing to do with Schlipal's death?"

"Beck was just the unfortunate soul who came upon Schlipal's body in the mess."

"But he worked in the same kitchen as Schlipal so who knows if he played a role in any of the pilfering?"

"I was a bit of an asshole to him," Neumann said.

Aachan smiled. "Just a bit?"

"He's not involved," Neumann said, ignoring the remark. "But I did leave the impression that I would come back with more questions about the pilfering."

"I see," Aachan said with a nod. "But maybe I'll go talk to him, put him a bit at ease."

"I'm not sure your presence would make him at ease. I'll probably send Knaup for that because he was there."

"Where is Corporal Knaup now?"

Neumann told him.

"He probably wasn't happy about that."

"I cleared that matter up."

Aachen smiled. "I'm sure you did." The smile disappeared. "There's something else we should look into about Chef Schlipal."

Neumann said nothing but gave indication that Aachen should continue. "You remember when we were investigating Mueller's death and you sent me to find out if Chef Schlipal was an informer for the Canadians?" Aachen paused, only continuing after Sergeant Neumann nodded. "I'm not sure if you remember, but I recall talking to a number of prisoners about what I was doing."

"Even though I told you not to tell anyone."

"They knew something was up so I had to tell them something."

"You could have lied."

"They would have seen through any lie." Aachen paused. "Should I continue with my information or would you rather just continue to berate me for something that happened months ago?"

"First tell me the names of these prisoners."

"Sergeant Olster and Corporals Tenefelde and Wissman."

"Boys from our area."

Aachen nodded.

"And probably having breakfast as we speak." Neumann waved for Aachen to continue with his story.

"And when I did find out that the chef was working with the Canadians," Aachen said, "those prisoners weren't pleased with the situation. They promised that they would have a discussion with Chef Schlipal and that it would be in my best interest not to interfere in this matter."

"Ah, I remember that now. You think that they did have this discussion with Schlipal and it got out of hand."

"It is in the realm of possibility, Sergeant. Olster definitely seemed keen to have a word with Schlipal."

Neumann nodded. But Aachen could see that the sergeant was distracted. "You have something else on your mind, don't you, Sergeant?"

After a few seconds, Neumann blinked and turned his attention to Aachen. "Yes Corporal Aachen, I have other thoughts and they are not pleasant."

"Do you wish to share these thoughts with me, or will you keep them to yourself so they can fester?"

"For the moment, I'll let them fester, Corporal Aachen."

"Is that wise, Sergeant? Last time you sat on your thoughts you were almost killed."

"There was little you could have done to help me, Aachen, because you were in the hospital at the time."

"I'm here now."

"Yes, but I think it's best for these not-very-pleasant thoughts to sit in my brain awhile to see if anything arises."

Aachen sighed in disappointment.

"But I do have a task in mind for you, Corporal."

"Of course, Sergeant. I'm always here to help."

Neumann nodded. "I want to find these three soldiers, Olster, Tenefelde and—"

"And Wissman," Aachen said, interrupting the sergeant and standing up. "You said they are probably having breakfast."

Neumann looked up at Aachen with slight smile. The corporal saw it and then blushed. "Sorry Sergeant, I'm starting to interrupt you again."

"No, no, Aachen. It shows that you're getting back to your old self again."

"Then I can interrupt you some more, if you like."

"Let's just see how that works out. But first, go find those three soldiers you mentioned and talk to them."

"Just me, Sergeant? You don't wish to interrogate them yourself?"

"If I talk to them, it will look like an interrogation. But if you do—"

"It won't," Aachen said, interrupting the sergeant again, but Neumann ignored it. "Well, not as much. They would know I was questioning them about Schlipal but they might talk more freely with me than you."

"You understand the situation well, Aachen." Neumann turned and lay back on his bed, putting his hands behind his head and shut his eyes.

Aachen stood for a moment looking down at the sergeant. Neumann felt his lingering presence and opened his eyes. "Is there anything else, Corporal Aachen?"

"Well, Sergeant," he paused, looking for words. "I was wondering what you'll be doing while I talk to Olster, Tenefelde, and Wissman?"

"You can rest easy, Corporal. I will not run headlong into Sergeant Heidfeld and his gang in their hut. That kind of forward movement needs more planning and you know me; I don't rush headlong into an enemy position by myself."

"You have done exactly that a number of times, Sergeant. Remember that British artillery position in Africa? You ran into that without warning them or us."

"That's what the situation called for, Aachen. An element of surprise for all involved. And need I remind you that I was not alone in that charge? I had you and the rest of the squad right behind me. You reacted the way I expected you to react." Neumann shut his eyes again.

Aachen shook his head. Without another word, he turned from the sergeant's bunk, grabbed his winter coat, and left.

After several moments, Neumann opened his eyes. He turned his head left and right, looking for Aachen. He slowly sat up, grunting softly in pain. He took a deep breath, thinking that the Schlipal situation had become more complicated, even more so since Aachen had reminded him about the chef's involvement with the Canadians and the camp's reaction to that. He shut his eyes and for the first time in a long time, Neumann felt like the tired, old soldier he actually was, not the tough squad leader that Aachen saw him as, who would rush headlong towards a British artillery position in the middle of a dust storm. He wanted nothing but for the war to end, regardless of who won, so he could go home where his duty would be to no one but himself. But he knew that was impossible at the moment. Despite the gains the Allies had made, the Führer would push back. And he'd push back hard and fast. It wouldn't win the war, only delay the ending and possibly create a situation to negotiate peace. This meant he might be able to go home soon.

But that was a long way away. Even if there wasn't a push, Germany would fight much harder to defend their borders and their homeland than France, Belgium, and Holland. Even the Russians would have a tough time fighting their way into Germany. The fighting would last another three, maybe even six, months. Neumann reluctantly stood up, grabbed his winter coat, and walked in the opposite direction that Aachen had gone.

7.

Aachen left the hut but instead of heading to the mess as planned, he circled back around. He would end up at the mess, but he had one more thing to do before he did.

He quickly and quietly jogged over to the neighbouring hut and dashed around the corner. Here he waited, with a view of the eastern door of his hut. He pulled his hood over his head and lit a cigarette. Aachen didn't smoke on a regular basis, but he wanted to blend in and to look just like any other prisoner who was outside to escape the noise and smell of the huts.

He waited, puffing the smoke out instead of inhaling it directly into his lungs. It wasn't until he'd almost finished the cigarette that his waiting paid off.

The side door of his hut opened and Sergeant Neumann stepped out. Aachen knew the sergeant was up to something other than a rest in his bunk. He wasn't disappointed that the sergeant hadn't told him the entire truth; Neumann was his superior and he didn't have to answer to anyone on his squad. But Neumann also felt the need to protect his squad, and Aachen thought that it was his turn to reciprocate.

He wouldn't let Neumann go looking for trouble without support.

The sergeant headed east between the huts, along a well-cleared path in the snow. Aachen followed, not directly behind, but one hut to north of him and kept track of his position through the spaces between the buildings.

Neumann walked hunched forward into the wind, not looking back to see if anybody was watching him. It was entirely possible that Neumann was aware that he was being followed. But if the sergeant knew, he didn't show it.

Once Neumann had passed a couple of the huts and continued southeast, Aachen realized where he was headed. He stopped and lit another cigarette. For a moment, he wondered if he should continue to follow because the sergeant was entering a dangerous area, not a place that welcomed most prisoners of the camp. But the events of the summer had changed a few things; there was more of a connection between the sergeant, with his role as head of Civil Security, and the men who lived in the hut where Neumann was heading. And Aachen knew Sergeant Neumann was quite adept at looking after himself.

Aachen finished his cigarette and headed towards the mess.

8.

The mess was starting to empty, although more slowly than usual. Prisoners leaving the building pushed past Aachen as they walked out, but there was no rush of prisoners coming in, as this was a last shift for breakfast. Many men lingered inside, not keen on going out into the cold. The last group to eat each meal was also responsible for cleaning the mess so many prisoners were collecting plates, bowls, and cutlery from the tables.

The tables themselves were made of wood, about two metres long with long benches on each side. Meals were served family style and each prisoner served themselves. The food was basic, though the cooks in the kitchen could be creative with the supplies they were given. This morning, the scrambled eggs had large chunks of ham throughout, a dish that Aachen remembered his grandmother cooking for him whenever he visited. The eggs were accompanied by bowls of toast, made from freshly baked bread, and plates of real butter that the prisoners could scrape on as thick as they liked.

For Aachen and many of the prisoners, the food in Camp 133 was the best they had eaten in the entire war. The eggs were real and they got meat at least once a day, sometimes more. And it was real meat like pork, beef, and chicken, not something made from a dead horse. Plus, they were given unlimited amounts of coffee, sugar, butter, and milk, food he knew was rationed for the Canadian civilians in the town next to the camp. Each prisoner was also given a carton of cigarettes a week, decent Canadian cigarettes, too.

No one in the war ate and smoked better than these German prisoners and the reasons were quite simple. The Canadians knew the German prisoners would be in touch with their families and friends back home as regular mail was also one of the requirements for POWs. So the Canadians figured that if they fed and treated their German prisoners well, then word of this would no doubt reach those in power back in Germany. They hoped it would result in reciprocal treatment of Canadians held by the Germans.

But Aachen knew that Germany did not have the agricultural resources, or the vast and unbombed landscape the Canadians did. So while the Canadian prisoners would be given enough food so they wouldn't completely starve, he knew they wouldn't get scrambled eggs with ham like Oma used to make with unlimited amounts of toast, butter, milk, and juice.

Even though this shift for breakfast was finished, there was still some food left over. Aachen grabbed two bowls of eggs and toast from one table and went from table to table, emptying the leftovers of other soldiers' meals into the bowls he carried until he was satisfied with the amount of food he collected.

He wove his way through the mess until he spotted who he was looking for. He walked over and sat down on the bench across from two soldiers, two corporals who had served in the same battalion as him in North Africa.

On the right was a former industrial worker name Christian Tenefelde and next to him was Karl Wissman, the stocky son of a coal miner. Tenefelde wore wire-rimmed glasses, while Wissman had a bent nose and some missing teeth. Both of them were originally from the Ruhr area, and both had flushed faces as if they had been doing some kind of exercise a few moments earlier.

Tenefelde smiled when Aachen sat down across from them. "Hey, Corporal Aachen. It's a fine morning for breakfast, don't you think?" Wissman frowned slightly, but still nodded in greeting.

Aachen placed the leftovers in the middle of the table and grabbed an unused bowl and a piece of toast. He reached across and took the knife next to Tenefelde's plate and used it to smear a thick layer of butter on his bread. Aachen looked the toast over for several seconds, like a scientist examining a specimen, and then took a bite. He closed his eyes as he savoured the taste. The other two prisoners watched him, smiling.

Aachen scooped some eggs with ham on top of his bread and took a bite of that. He sighed a deeply contented sigh.

"It is a fine breakfast, I'll give you that. I still can't believe that we get to eat as much butter as we like," Aachen said, patting his stomach. "Probably not good for my belly, but Dr. Kleinjeld said I should eat more and who am I to disagree with the good doctor?"

"Kleinjeld says I've been eating too much butter," Wissman said with a huff. "He says too much butter is bad for my heart. But I told him he didn't complain about how bullets and artillery fire were bad for my heart in Africa."

"Yeah, it's funny how the doctors worry about saving our lives now that we're in a place where we can't get hurt," Tenefelde said. But a second later, he flushed, realizing the mistake of his words.

They both set down their utensils, their faces serious. "We're very glad to see both you and the sergeant out and about on your usual duties, Klaus," Wissman said with much sincerity.

"You bet," Tenefelde added with a series of quick nods. "When I saw you getting trampled about by the crowd after the wrestling match last summer, I thought you were done for. And when I heard how the sergeant was beaten, I couldn't believe it. Who attacks someone with sandbags? I mean, we all know who did, but what a terrible ordeal that must have been."

Tenefelde went back to eating, oblivious to his bunk-mate's incredulous stare. After a moment of awkward silence Tenefelde glanced up and saw the two other corporals looking at him. "What?" he asked. "Is there something wrong?"

Wissman used the back of his hand to slap Tenefelde on the forearm.

"Ouch!"

"You're a bit of an idiot, aren't you, Christian?"

"What? I was the top of my class in my village, you know."

"The top for what, village idiot?"

"Science and mathematics, which is why I worked in the appliance factory while you slaved away underground in a coal mine."

"I wasn't underground. I was the assistant to the executive assistant of the vice president."

"So you were assistant to the assistant of the head assistant?" Tenefelde said with a laugh. "Good to know you had an important position under such an important person."

This banter went back and forth for several minutes and Aachen ate his breakfast, waiting for lull in the conversation. He wanted to interrupt them but watching Sergeant Neumann these past several months had taught him to be patient. Many of Neumann's interrogations began informally, so much like a normal conversation that many people had no idea they were being interrogated. Neumann could be hard and tough if he needed to be, but it was his casual and relaxed attitude towards people that put them at ease and caused them to let their guard down. Aachen figured he would attempt Neumann's strategy and see where it would take him with these two.

There was a break in the banter and Aachen asked, "You no doubt heard the news?" He tried his best to make it seem like an offhand remark. Yet when Tenefelde and Wissman froze, looked at each other, then to Aachen with the same quizzical expression, he figured he might have pushed it too soon.

"You haven't heard?"

"Did we win the war?" Tenefelde asked. His question seemed so serious that it confused Aachen. But when Tenefelde and Wissman broke out in laughter, Aachen realized it was only a joke.

Wissman gave Tenefelde a jocular punch on the arm. "Good one Chris. Did we win the war? That's rich."

Tenefelde laughed even more, glad that his joke got a great response. Aachen smiled and attempted a slight chuckle but it was forced. Still, the others didn't notice. They were still laughing about the joke, which Aachen found very interesting. As near as a month or so ago, no one would have joked about the war or made a sarcastic remark about the German army. Or speculated too much about when the fighting would end, or question whether Germany would win. Such remarks would have been traitorous, even punishable by death.

But since the Allies had advanced all the way to the German border, hardly anyone still believed that Germany would win. The prevailing feeling in the camp was that the war would end some way in the next few months and the Führer and his ilk would be deposed of, so there was no worry about saying things out loud that a lot of the men had only quietly thought about for months.

Despite his unquiet about the joke, Aachen was grateful for how it distracted them from his forced comment.

"Sorry we missed the end of the war, Klaus. We were out playing hockey this morning," Wissman said.

"Hockey?" Aachen asked. "In this weather?" He was naturally curious but he also realized that this might be a nice way to let the conversation flow, to see if the boys accidentally offered any other unintended information about their dealings with Schlipal that might be connected to his death.

"Ice hockey, I mean," Wissman added.

"You know, that crazy Canadian sport with skates and sticks," said Tenefelde. "It's very exciting."

"Technically, it's not a Canadian sport. I think it was invented by the Brits, a kind of winter version of field hockey. But the Canadians are crazy about it and say it's their national sport."

"You played ice hockey?" Aachen asked. "In Germany?"

Tenefelde shook his head vigorously. "No, no. I didn't play back home. I learned from a couple of the Canadian scouts last winter. After we all got settled in the camp, I was getting bored with sitting around and didn't want to learn a new trade or walk in circles around the edge of camp over and over again like many of the prisoners did. I wanted to do something fun. My uncle had taught me how to skate back home, so when I saw the Canadians flooding part of the camp to make some ice, I got some skates from sporting supplies. I think someone from the town donated them for us.

"I was on the ice when a few scouts came out with a bunch of hockey sticks and pucks, and started playing. They were so fast. I must have been staring because one of the scouts came over and handed me a stick. He handed a bunch of other prisoners sticks—"

"I got one, too," Wissman interrupted.

"Yeah, he got one, and then the Canadians showed us how to play. It was exactly what I was looking for. Crazy, like going into battle but no one gets killed."

"Last year was just practice but this year we started a league with different huts. Since the season begins in a few days, we've been practicing." Wissman said.

"This morning?" Aachen asked.

"Ice is much better in the morning when it's cold," Wissman replied. "It starts to get soft and mushy as the day warms up."

"Although that will probably be less of an issue here since the Canadian winter is much colder than back home."

"Wasn't it too dark to play?" Aachen asked.

They shrugged. "It was civil twilight; not a lot of light but we used to go into battle with less light many times, remember?" Tenefelde said. "But some of the Canadian tower guards turned their spotlights on the rink so there was plenty of light to see."

Aachen was surprised by that. There was a high guard tower every hundred metres or so along the perimeter of the camp, twenty-two in total, with spotlights and sharpshooters with shoot-to-kill orders for any prisoner who crossed into the twenty-metre-wide no man's land that encircled the camp's interior perimeter.

For some of these guards to shine their spotlights so a bunch of prisoners could see better while playing hockey seemed to be a total lack of discipline from the Veterans Guards. The Canadians were not known for such lax behaviour, especially while on duty. When Aachen mentioned that, Tenefelde and Wissman just shrugged.

"The war's going to be over in a few months so no one's planning to escape," Tenefelde said. "And the Canadians know it."

Again, Aachen was a bit surprised because this was the second time these German prisoners had openly talked about the end of the war without worrying about being overheard and charged with treason.

"And it was only practice so were just skating around, passing the puck, working on some strategic moves," added Wissman, "so we didn't need The Butcher."

"The butcher?" asked Aachen. "Is that a special position? I don't know much about the sport."

Wissman and Tenefelde both laughed. "He thinks the butcher is a position in ice hockey."

"Considering how the Canadians use their sticks, he could be right." They laughed some more.

After a moment, Wissman turned to Aachen. "The Butcher is just our goalkeeper."

"Olster," Tenefelde said. "You remember him? Used to be a butcher back home. You wrestled him a couple of times before your match with Neuer in July."

Aachen nodded. "Yeah, I remember Olster." He also remembered it was Olster who said that Schlipal would be dealt with for working with the Canadians in some kind of black market scheme. But Aachen deliberately did not mention this.

"He blocks the goal, like in football. He's big which is very helpful," said Wissman.

"And he's stubborn so it's hard to get anything past him. And a bit dirty, as you might expect, so if you get too close, he'll come after you." Wissman continued.

"Yes, Olster did have some questionable tactics when we wrestled," Aachen said.

"Which makes him perfect for ice hockey," said Tenefelde. "The game, we've learned, is quite open to 'questionable tactics.' Especially the way the Canadians play. We played an exhibition game with some of them, 'shinny' they called it, and I still have the bruises from all the errant elbows and stick slashes."

"After that game, I was really glad we never went into battle against the Canadians," Wissman added. "If those old Veterans Guards are so tough and dirty just playing hockey, imagine how tough and dirty they would be on the battlefield."

"So you had a practice this morning," Aachen said as casually as he could, "but your regular goalkeeper Olster wasn't there."

Tenefelde nodded while Wissman shook his head.

"We thought he'd be there, but he wasn't," Wissman said. "But it wasn't a problem because we weren't practicing shooting on he goal, so I guess it made sense that he didn't show up."

Aachen nodded, pretending this information wasn't important though he knew it was. Sergeant Neumann would probably want to know this. And then it would best if the two of them talked to Olster. The butcher was slow moving but not dim-witted. Once he realized that Schlipal had been killed, he would know he would be a suspect.

After a moment, Aachen realized that the two corporals on the other side of the table were staring at him. "Is there any gambling involved in these games?" he asked, pretending to do his job so he wouldn't mention his suspicions about Olster.

Tenefelde and Wissman looked at each, reluctant to respond.

"Come on fellows. You're in the hockey league so Sergeant Neumann is going to wonder. It's best that you tell me outright instead of having him talk to you about it. You know how he is."

A quick look passed between the two soldiers, followed by a nod from Tenefelde. "But it's not something we're involved in since we play on a team," Wissman said. "It'd be improper."

"Although we were asked if we would be part of this gambling network," Tenefelde added with a sneer. "They said we could make some money if we held back during some parts of our games, kept the score close."

"Or even lose," Wissman said with the same disdain. "We told those fuckers to fuck off."

"What fuckers?" Aachen asked.

"One of those assholes from Heidfeld's group in Hut 14," Tenefelde said. "Can't recall his name. Some jerk who used to be in Camp 130 in that Medicine place, whatever it's called."

"Medicine Hat," said Aachen. The man Tenefelde was talking about was named Sergeant Konrad, a recent transfer from Camp 130. Nominally, Konrad was the hut leader for #14 but probably a deputy of some type to Heidfeld in his black market organization. Aachen had only met Konrad once, when the man and some others beat him and tried to hang him in the shower in the summer. They did not succeed. "I was approached in the same way by Sergeant Heidfeld himself last summer. He asked me to let Neuer win our match. Said I would be compensated and that I should look to the future."

"What did you tell him?" Tenefelde asked. The other corporals looked at him with surprise. "Oh yeah. Sorry."

"So I guess the answer is yes, there is gambling on the hockey and it looks like Heidfeld is trying to fix the games," said Aachen.

The other two nodded. "There's gambling on everything in this camp," Wissman added with a shrug.

"There was even a bet going on for whether or not you would survive, whether you would walk again. Even on how many ribs Sergeant Neumann had broken."

Wissman slapped Tenefelde across the shoulder again. "Jesus, Chris, do you have no means in your brain to hold some of your words back?"

And the bickering banter began again, but Aachen ignored them. He was thinking about Olster and fighting the urge to sprint from the room to tell Neumann what he'd found out. But if he did that the boys would be suspicious, so he continued to slowly finish his breakfast.

9.

Neumann paused for a moment outside the door of the legionnaire hut, took a deep breath, and walked in. As he waited at the door for his eyes to adjust to the dim interior light, two large prisoners approached him.

Unlike the previous times he appeared in this hut, the two soldiers did not threaten him. But they did block him from going further.

"Is there something we can help you with, Sergeant Neumann?" the prisoner on the right asked. His name was Sergeant Hans Forst. His tone was respectful but also circum-spect, the way a border guard would greet someone returning home from a faraway location. At least the way a border guard would treat someone during a time of peace.

"I would like to see Colonel Ehrhoff." Neumann responded with a similar tone, respectful but all business. Ehrhoff was the commander of this hut, which was inhabited completely by legionnaires, German soldiers who had been members of the French Foreign Legion but were then amalgamated into the Wehrmacht during the early part of the war. Despite their German heritage, many other German soldiers viewed the legionnaires with suspicion because of what they believed to be dual loyalties. This was the reason the legionnaires had their own hut and mostly kept to themselves.

Neumann understood the suspicious feelings on both sides because, to many legionnaires, their oath to the Legion some-times seemed stronger than their feelings for their homeland. But he also knew the legionnaires had fought well for the Fatherland, even better in some cases because of their training and experience. And the Allies made no distinctions in battle between regular German soldiers and German legionnaires. They killed both with just as much fervour so, in the end, Neumann really didn't care. If you fought hard for Germany, he would treat you with respect. Hell, he even respected many of the Canadians guarding the camp because even though they were enemy soldiers, they, like him, had fought hard in the Great War and had lost friends in battle.

"May I ask the reasons for your request?" Forst asked.

"You may ask, Sergeant Forst, but this is something I would prefer to discuss with Colonel Ehrhoff privately."

The two guards looked at him for a few seconds and then Forst nodded. "Go tell Colonel Ehrhoff that Sergeant Neumann would like to talk to him," he said without moving his gaze from Neumann.

The other guard, a legionnaire named Sergeant Phillip Schuchardt, turned on his heel and went to pass the request on to Colonel Ehrhoff.

Forst and Neumann stood in silence for several moments. Neumann was the first to break it.

"How is your family, Sergeant Forst?" Since his dealings with the legionnaires did not get off to a great start during the events of the summer, he had done some research into the backgrounds of some of the soldiers with whom there had been conflict. Forst was one of them—they had briefly scuffled and afterwards, Neumann had learned that the sergeant had a family in North Africa, a wife and a son.

The legionnaire was briefly taken aback by the question but quickly recovered. "They're doing fine," he replied.

"They're having no difficulty now that the Allies are in charge?"

"They are being treated well."

"At least there's no fighting anymore."

"Yes. I'm glad they are now a good distance from the war."

"That's always good." Neumann said nothing after this, letting the silence linger.

"My son, however," continued Forst, "is being bullied by some of the children on the street."

"Children can be cruel sometimes."

"Yes, but he is a strong boy so he fights back well."

"Much like his father."

The look on Forst's face showed that he wasn't sure how to take that comment. Neumann knew that Forst was trying to determine if it was a compliment or an insult since Neumann had bested him during their altercation in the summer. Neumann let Sergeant Forst struggle with that for a moment before changing the subject.

"Will you go back to Germany after the war?" he casually asked.

Again, the legionnaire was surprised by the question. It took him a moment to filter it, dismiss the previous comment, and respond to this one. "I will go wherever the Legion orders me to serve."

Neumann nodded but held back any comments about where the Legion would serve next, and any questions about whether Forst thought Indochina was going to be a problem for the French after the war. While he respected the legionnaires, he couldn't understand their desire to continually return to battle after years and years of war and all its horrors. He understood the importance of fighting for one's country but to continue to fight in other battles when the war ended, either as a mercenary or by joining the highly respected Legion, was anathema to him.

The other guard, Schuchardt, returned. "Colonel Ehrhoff has agreed to talk to you, Sergeant Neumann," he said. "If you'd follow me."

"Excellent," said Neumann. Before he made his way deeper into the hut, Neumann nodded to Forst. "All the best to you, Sergeant. I hope for the best for your son and wife."

Forst nodded, ignoring the odd look his partner gave him. Neumann gestured to other legionnaire. "Please, Sergeant Schuchardt, take me to Colonel Ehrhoff."

The walk took only a few minutes. When they arrived, Neumann was shocked by the change in the hut since the last time he was here. During the summer, Ehrhoff had set up a large tent with a carpet on the floor and filled it with pillows to sit on. At the time, the colonel had declared his deep respect for the Bedouins of the desert and aped their ways. He even dressed like a Bedouin.

But the tent and the pillows were gone. The carpet was still on the floor but it was now under a simple desk and armchair, with two basic stacking chairs in front. Ehrhoff was in the armchair writing in a notebook. He had also eschewed the Bedouin robes for his proper uniform. That is, his legionnaire uniform rather than his Wehrmacht one.

Sergeant Schuchardt cleared his throat to get Ehrhoff's attention. The colonel looked up and both Schuchardt and Neumann snapped to attention and saluted. Ehrhoff saluted back. "Sergeant Neumann," he said like a factory owner greeting a respected worker. "How are you on this cold day?"

"I am doing fine," Neumann said, remaining at attention.

"Please sit, Sergeant."

Neumann nodded, pulled his coat off, draped it over his forearm, and sat down. He kept his posture erect as he sat.

"That will be all, Phillip," Ehrhoff said to Schuchardt, who hesitated but saluted and walked away.

Once Schuchardt had moved beyond earshot, Ehrhoff put his pen down and gave Neumann his full attention. "You are doing well, Sergeant Neumann? You have recovered from your injuries?"

Neumann nodded. "For the most part. Although I think the weather will play havoc with my bones in my old age."

"That is a terrible shame. I'm sorry we were unable to help earlier in that situation."

"Your man, Poulson, saved my life and for that, Colonel Ehrhoff, I'm eternally grateful."

"Again, we should have acted earlier." There was a pause. Neumann knew there was nothing really more to say about this subject and could see that Ehrhoff felt the same way. He wanted to move the conversation forward but also knew that Ehrhoff was the kind of superior officer who liked to initiate things on his own. Ehrhoff was a decent officer but, like many older officers from the first war, a bit pompous. The monocle hanging from his pocket didn't help matters.

"So, I was told you wish to talk to me and I suspect this is not a personal visit."

"Yes, Colonel, I'm here in my role as the head of Civil Security and must inform you that there has been another death similar to Captain Mueller's."

"Another one!?" Ehrhoff failed to contain his surprise. "Another hanging?"

Neumann shook his head. "A little different this time, but clearly murder."

"Who is the poor victim?"

"Captain Schlipal," replied Neumann. He added nothing else because he wished to see how Ehrhoff reacted to the name. Neumann didn't suspect that Ehrhoff was involved in this situation—he had come to the Legion commander for another reason—but the old village policeman in him couldn't help himself.

The look on Ehrhoff's face was confusion. It was obvious he had heard the name but was trying to place it. "Schlipal," he said after a moment. "I don't know that man. He's not a legionnaire, is he?"

"He was not. He was the head chef for Mess # 3."

"Then I don't understand why you are here to see me since our chef is Major Walter and this Schlipal was never in the Legion."

"I'm here for another reason, Colonel," Neumann said quietly. "I am looking for some assistance."

"I don't think I can provide you with assistance in this matter. It has no connection to me or the men in our hut."

"Which is why I need your assistance, Colonel. You see, Captain Schlipal was also involved in a black market scheme with some others inside and outside the camp that involved pilfering from his kitchen."

Ehrhoff clicked his tongue in disgust. "I don't understand this kind of mentality. Profiting off your fellow soldiers, especially during a time of war?"

"War is the best time for profiteering, Colonel. There are so many materials moving around that it's hard to keep track of them. And with plenty of rationing in the civilian section, there is much demand for certain items—so much so that people will pay a much higher price for these luxuries. There's plenty of money to be made, on all sides."

"It's still disgusting, especially when people in this camp

worry about us being disloyal to Germany when there are so-called 'good Germans' back home doing the same thing to our own people."

Neumann shrugged and held back any comments about Germans doing far worse things to their own people in a time of war. "Be that as it may, Colonel, one of my suspicions about Schlipal's death may be connected to those inside the camp who deal in the black market and other unsavoury activities."

"Yes, Sergeant Heidfeld and his friends," Ehrhoff said. "He's made many attempts to corrupt my men. And though I have pride in my legionnaires, they are, in the end, only men in the middle of a prisoner-of-war camp with little to do. For some, the temptation is difficult to resist."

"There's little one can do to completely stop such things, Colonel, as I well know. The trick is knowing which battles to fight, which vices are relatively harmless, at least in moderation."

"Yes, I agree with you, Sergeant. But that doesn't explain why you need my assistance."

Neumann leaned forward in his chair and spoke in a quiet voice, soft enough not to be heard by anyone trying to listen in, but loud enough for Ehrhoff to hear. "There will come a time during my investigation when I will have to approach Sergeant Heidfeld. And I'm pretty sure he will not be pleased and will order his men to respond, probably with violence. They have done so before. It would make this situation easier if I knew the Legion would assist me."

"We're not bodyguards, Sergeant Neumann. We're an army of soldiers. Proud soldiers, not mercenaries."

"And that's why I need you. Heidfeld's men are mostly mercenaries and if they knew that I had the support of an army of soldiers such as yours, then they wouldn't be so quick to resort to violence."

"You already have an army behind you, Sergeant. There are many men in this camp who support you."

"I would like to have more. Some of these fellows, especially Heidfeld, only understand power."

"You're the head of Civil Security in this camp, Sergeant Neumann, you have the power of the Führer and the whole nation of Germany behind you."

"That power is fading as the war moves on, Colonel. There are now people who are looking to other powerful leaders in this confusing time. And Sergeant Heidfeld is becoming one. You know that. You said so yourself that he was attempting and succeeding in corrupting some of your men."

Ehrhoff leaned back in his chair and clasped his hands together in front of him. Neumann saw that he was thinking the proposal over. And he knew better than to try to be more convincing. He had made his point to Ehrhoff and the colonel would either agree or he would not.

Finally, Ehrhoff spoke. "You make some good points, Neumann, although I'm not sure what I can do for you. I'll let it be known amongst my legionnaires that I support your work in this camp, that I look down on corruption in the camp, that I look down on stealing from our own countrymen, and that they should assist you in any way they see fit. I leave it to them to decide the means."

"Thank you, sir. That will help me."

Since there was little left to say, Neumann stood at attention, saluted the colonel, and left.

10.

Aachen considered returning to his hut to tell the sergeant about Olster not showing up for hockey practice, but thought better of it. He decided to see if he could find Olster himself. Aachen figured the butcher had his own reasons for missing practice, but something about how Wissman and Tenefelde talked about him gave Aachen an uneasy feeling.

As he walked over to Olster's hut, with his head bent against the cold wind, Aachen contemplated what he knew about Olster and determined that he wasn't the type to kill someone unless it was in the heat of battle. Or, at least, he didn't think he was. Both Aachen and Sergeant Neumann were completely taken by surprise by who killed Captain Mueller in the summer. The sergeant paid a hefty price for his oversight.

There was the possibility that Olster had approached Chef Schlipal to confront him about working with Canadian black marketeers and the encounter had got out of hand. But why would he have waited several months to do so? The butcher had plenty of time in the summer and fall to exact some kind of punishment. Especially between the months of August and October when both Aachen and Sergeant Neumann were recovering from their injuries and no one had filled the Civil Security role in their absence.

That would have been the perfect time for Olster to accost the chef. Prisoners of the more criminal variety, especially Sergeant Heidfeld, had taken advantage of that time, expanding their networks of gambling, black marketing, and other nefarious activities in the camp. So much so that it was proving difficult to keep these offenders under control because their networks were so large. It didn't help that most of the prisoners knew the war would soon be over, that Germany would lose. Discipline and morale were lacking. Heidfeld had taken advantage of that and was becoming one of the big power brokers in the camp.

Aachen thought this was probably why Sergeant Neumann suspected that Heidfeld was involved in Schlipal's death, but was also reluctant to approach him outright. Even before Heidfeld had gained so much power, he was quite willing to use violence, as Aachen had experienced firsthand that summer.

Even if he found the butcher, it wouldn't be an overly pleasant experience. Olster was a cantankerous person, quick to anger, willing to hold a grudge. He had faced the man twice on the wrestling mat since they arrived in the camp. There was no doubt that Olster was strong and not fond of losing. He was known for employing wrestling techniques that weren't entirely illegal in matches, but were seen by many as unsports-manlike. Aachen found that the best way to defeat someone like Olster on the mat was to ignore the taunts and the objectionable moves and take him down as quickly as possible.

The corporal entered Olster's hut and climbed up to the second floor where he knew the butcher had his bunk. It was about a third of the way down the fourth row. Olster was not there. His bunk, though, was well-kept and tidy, which surprised Aachen because the butcher wasn't known for his personal hygiene. Still, military training and years of battlefield experience probably played a role here. Aachen served with many soldiers who didn't care what they looked or smelled like, but were extremely fastidious about their pack and their weapons. For the most part, good hygiene was difficult to maintain in battle and infrequent bathing didn't usually get someone killed the way a neglected weapon would.

Aachen thought about searching Olster's pack, but held back. So far, the butcher was innocent of anything so it didn't feel right to rifle through his personal effects. A prisoner a few bunks over saw Aachen standing there.

"If you're looking for the Butcher, Corporal Aachen, he's not here," the prisoner shouted over. He was sitting on a lower bunk, knitting a pair of winter socks. Although this man recognized Aachen, the corporal did not know him. This was not surprising since there were over 12,000 prisoners in Camp 133 and Aachen was known as Sergeant Neumann's assistant and as a noted wrestler. Aachen gave up wrestling when he was seriously injured after defeating Kriegsmarine Lieutenant Neuer to win the camp heavyweight championship that past summer.

"Have you seen him lately?" Aachen asked calmly, slowly walking over to the bunk. He didn't want to spook the prisoner by giving him the impression that Olster might be in trouble.

"Olster do something wrong?" the prisoner asked with a smile.

Aachen smiled back, trying not to give away his surprise at the prisoner's reaction. "No, not really. Some of the boys are discussing starting the wrestling club back up again and I wanted to see if Sergeant Olster would consider helping out."

The prisoner's eyes widened. "You're going to wrestle again? After what happened last summer?"

Aachen shook his head. "No. Not me. My body isn't healed enough to start that again. However, since some of the other lads were talking about it, I said I was willing to coach. I'm looking for Olster to see if he'd help."

"Oh yeah, he'd be a real nurturing coach," the prisoner said with a laugh. Aachen chuckled back.

"I have to ask. He's got plenty of experience on the mat."

"Yeah, I can see that. Now that I think about it, when he left here, he was grumbling something about hiding out in the exercise room, I think."

Aachen nodded, knowing that Olster probably meant the wrestling training room which was largely unused since Aachen's match with Neuer in July. It was located in the north end of one of the smaller classrooms at the end of Row 5. It was a relatively quiet building that the wrestlers had shared with some fencers. They were the only group in the building since they both needed some decent space to train.

"Oh, did he seem agitated or something?" It was a reflexive question and as soon as it came out of this mouth, Aachen knew it wasn't a smart thing to have asked.

The prisoner gave him a quizzical look. "You sure he's not in any trouble?"

Aachen waved a hand in assurance. "No, no. I'm trying to gauge the sergeant's mood. If he's agitated, then maybe today's not the day to approach him."

"The Butcher is always agitated about something so I'm not sure when is a good time to approach him," the prisoner said. "For the most part, I usually stay out of his way."

Aachen nodded. "Thanks for your help. I'll go look for him in the exercise room."

"Are you sure Olster isn't in trouble?" the soldier asked again. After a pause, he continued, "The only reason I ask is that you're not the first person to come looking for him in the last day or so."

Aachen did his best to mask his surprise. He especially tried to keep his voice even when he asked the prisoner who these visitors were.

"Just some idiots from Sergeant Heidfeld's gang—one of them was called Konrad, I think. They wanted to talk to The Butcher about hockey. Can you believe it? That son of a bitch is a goaltender for a team in the new league."

"I heard about that," Aachen said, wondering why someone

from Sergeant Heidfeld's group wanted to talk about hockey with Olster. Were they feeling him out for gambling purposes the same way they approached Tenefelde and Wissman? Was this happening all over the camp because of hockey? It was information he would bring up with Olster once he found him. And maybe with Sergeant Neumann because it might have something to do with Chef Schlipal's murder. "But I only want to talk to Sergeant Olster about wrestling. If he was in any kind of trouble, Sergeant Neumann would have been here instead of just me."

The prisoner accepted the lie and Aachen gave his thanks and said goodbye.

He quickly made his way to the training room. The building seemed empty when Aachen entered; there were no sounds of fencers bouncing off the floor or grunts from wrestlers in close combat. He waited for several minutes, allowing his eyes to adjust to the interior light.

The building was cold. Not as cold as outside, but pretty close. That meant no one had been inside for a while to light one of the two wooden stoves which heated the space. It felt like coming into a house that had been abandoned for months.

Once his eyes adjusted to the light, Aachen walked down the hallway, past the fencers' room to the one used by the wrestlers. He tried to push the door open but something was blocking it. He was able to get the door slightly ajar and peeked inside. There was a pile of weights and medicine balls stacked on the other side. He put his shoulder against the door and shoved, opening it just enough so he could squeeze through. He could have pushed harder and cleared all the debris from the entrance, but even opening the door by half a metre had caused his back muscles to seize up uncomfortably.

The room was dark and all the window blinds were closed. Save for the gear piled by the door—he wasn't sure why this was done or who had done it—it was exactly like it had been the last time he was here. Mats were stacked along the walls as they normally were after practice. The weight area, with its benches, weights, and other bits of equipment, stood along the other side of the room. Most of the equipment had been donated by various Canadian companies or sporting groups who were keen to show their Canadian kindness to the German prisoners, while also hoping the physical activity would keep them too busy to consider escaping from the camp. All the equipment in the camp, from the sporting goods and musical instruments, to the work tools and machines, had been donated for these reasons. And for the most part, it worked. Only a few prisoners had tried to escape in the time Aachen had been in the camp and all of them had been caught within a couple of days. In the last two months, no attempts had been made.

Aachen stepped into the room, wishing he had a flashlight. He decided to slowly make his way across the space—hoping not to trip over some piece of equipment—and bring up a window blind or two.

He got about a third of the way across the room when he heard a scuffle of feet behind him. He tried to turn to see who it was, but he felt an arm close around his neck before he had the chance. It was a thick, muscular arm that smelled strongly of sweat. Another arm pressed against the back of his head in a classic choke move. Because of the matches they'd had during the championship tournament, Aachen knew exactly who was applying the hold. The hand was covered in scar tissue from years of cutting meat.

"Olster," Aachen grunted as the arm squeezed tightly around his neck, cutting off his breath. He slapped at the arm, tried to pry it from him with his hands but the hold was too strong. Aachen tried to drop as a means to escape but Olster seemed ready for that too. Aachen fought hard to escape, using every move he could think of, but Olster was a veteran of thousands of wrestling matches and managed to keep the hold. As the grip grew tighter and his head grew lighter, Aachen knew that prior to that summer, he would have easily broken out of this hold. But he had suffered terrible injuries in the riot and was still a long way from being in top shape.

He was trapped. Olster's thick, butcher's arm squeezed tighter and tighter. Aachen's lungs screamed for oxygen and struggling only made it worse.

Before he blacked out, a surge of anger and regret flooded Aachen's mind. Anger at surviving all those battles in North Africa, even those months on the Eastern Front, in Stalingrad of all places, only to be killed by a sweaty butcher in a Canadian prisoner-of-war camp. And regret that he would never see his parents again.

11.

Aachen woke to the harsh smell of ammonia. The chemical scent burned his eyes, causing him to gasp and suck air deep into his lungs. That brought in more ammonia, more burning, more gasping. His shook his head, trying to clear the scent, and realized where the ammonia was coming from. He'd seen many wrestlers knocked out during a match and had been revived from the black a few times himself.

Smelling salts. Someone was waving them under his nose. And though the fumes were bothersome, at least it meant he was still alive. Olster hadn't choked the life out of him, only enough to render him unconscious.

Aachen batted away the hand waving the smelling salts. The ammonia faded and he heard the person move away. Aachen's vision was still blurry from the lack of oxygen. And he had a throbbing headache.

"Thought I killed you," a familiar voice said.

"Thought you killed me—" Aachen suddenly connected the voice to its owner. "Olster!" he shouted out loud. Adrenaline flooded Aachen's body and he was instantly awake.

His vision cleared slightly and he could see the silhouette of the butcher squatting on his haunches, leaning over him. Instinctively, Aachen struck out with his left hand, catching Olster with an open hand across the chin.

"Fuck," the butcher grunted. The force of the hit threw off his balance and sent him crashing to the floor.

Aachen pushed with his legs and scrambled backwards, trying to get as much distance from the butcher as he could. He tumbled over various pieces of discarded weight equipment, grabbing the handle of a mop that was used to clear sweat off the mats. He waved the mop in Olster's direction to keep the butcher from attacking him again.

But Olster only pushed himself to a seated position, rubbing his chin with his hand. "Still pretty fast, aren't you Aachen?" he said. "Although not as fast as you used to be. There was no way you'd have let me rush up on you from behind like that a few months ago."

"Fuck you, Olster," Aachen said, waving the mop again. But he could feel his arms getting tired.

"Although that's probably to be expected considering you got trampled by half the men in camp," Olster said. He still hadn't moved from his seated position. "I thought you were dead after that but I guess they make 'em stronger where you come from, huh? You're not some fucking weak city boy, I'll give you that."

Aachen kept the mop up but was confused. Why didn't Olster attack him again? Why did he revive him if he was trying to kill him? It made no sense. "You tried to kill me," Aachen said.

"Bah, if I wanted to kill you, you'd be fucking dead," Olster said, waving a hand. "I just thought you were one of those motherfucking assholes coming after me again. I was going to show them that Olster the Butcher is nobody to mess with. Leave one of them dead on the floor as a message to leave me alone. But just my fucking luck, you show up and I almost kill you."

"You weren't trying to kill me?"

"Weren't you listening to me? Of course I was trying to kill you. But I thought you were someone else. When I saw it was you, I let you go. Of course, you were fucking out by then, but you were alive."

Because Olster had revived Aachen with the smelling salts and had not made any threatening moves towards him since then, Aachen let his arms relax and lowered the mop. He did, however, keep a firm grip on it, just to be prepared.

"You said someone's been after you," Aachen said slowly, the fear tempering, allowing him to catch his breath. "Who?"

"Just some assholes who've been bothering me for the past week or so," Olster said, tossing the smelling salts across the room. "That's why I'm hiding out here. To get away from them."

"Why would anyone bother you?" Aachen said. "Nothing personal, Olster, but you're not that important in the camp."

"Fuck you, Aachen. Next time I won't hold back and I really will kill you."

"There won't be a next time between you and me like that, Olster."

The butcher laughed. "You're not the man you used to be, Aachen. And the camp's different now. If I can sneak up on you like I did, you'd better be careful because there are assholes out there that are a lot more dangerous than me."

"You're talking about Sergeant Heidfeld, aren't you?" Aachen said. Olster nodded. "You don't have to worry about him or his men. Sergeant Neumann and I will deal with them soon."

"Neumann isn't the man he used to be either," Olster said plainly. "He's gotten old, and not just in age. What happened with the general in the summer hit him harder than you think. It hit a lot of us hard. The war, too. All those assholes who tried to kill Hitler so they could get a negotiated peace. Fuck them. Because of that, more corrupt bastards are coming out of the woodwork, even here. Especially here 'cause we can't do anything about the war. I hoped that Sergeant Heidfeld himself would come after me, but that fucker never gets his own hands dirty. Always get someone else to do his work for him."

"But why is Sergeant Heidfeld after you?

Olster looked around, trying to avoid answering the question. But Aachen let the silence stew, using Sergeant Neumann's technique of saying nothing to force the other person to fill the uncomfortable quiet.

"Fucking hockey," Olster said at last. "I knew I should have said no to those fuckers, kept out of these stupid sports they keep pushing on us. It was kind of fun. I didn't have to do much, just stand there, let a couple of pucks bounce off me and hit anyone that came close with my stick. I didn't think it would get like it has."

"It's just a game."

"You're completely unfit to deal with any of the assholes in this camp if you think that. It's like the wrestling, the football, the cards, the dates the war will end, all that kind of shit that—"

"The gambling," Aachen interrupted the butcher.

"The gambling," Olster repeated. "And other things."

"They're trying to rig the games, right?"

Olster nodded. "How did you know?"

"Last summer, Heidfeld approached me himself, asked me to let Neuer win our match. I told him to fuck off. So that night, he sent a bunch of his thugs and they beat me up in the shower so I couldn't wrestle. I got a few licks in but there were six of them. They even tried to hang me but I got lucky so they didn't kill me."

Olster raised an eyebrow. "When did this happen?"

"Not long before Neuer and I fought. A few days, I think. It's hard to remember details now."

Olster whistled in appreciation. "And you still managed to beat that big fucking submariner? You're a tough little shit, aren't you?"

"Still am. And since I faced Heidfeld and his jerks once before, I'll be ready for them again."

"It's a bit different this time," Olster said, looking around as if somebody was listening. His voice went quiet. "This time they've got the Canadians involved."

"Canadians? Like some guards?"

Olster nodded and Aachen was surprised. The Veterans Guards were usually honourable. Tough, but honourable. To hear that some might be involved with Heidfeld was concerning. "Why would guards be involved?"

"The war's ending so the lines between enemies are fading," Olster said with a shrug. "And it's hockey. The Canadians love hockey and because of the war there isn't a lot of local hockey going on. So when they heard about a league in the camp they wanted to get in on the gambling side. And that's why Heidfeld is trying to rig some games. So he can make more and take more home when the war ends."

"He won't be able to take much home when they repatriate us."

"He will if he gets some Canadians involved. He'll get them to send him whatever he's made once the war is over. They'll take a share, but they'll give him enough."

Aachen shook his head at the audacity of Sergeant Heidfeld. Olster was right about one thing: this thing was too big for Aachen. Sergeant Neumann understood the criminal mind, which was why he was a good investigator. And why he did the job at home. But Aachen didn't have the stomach for it, and he was realizing that law enforcement was not the path he would choose after the war.

Still, he had one more question for Olster. "What about Schlipal?"

Aachen saw a look of panic pass over Olster's face. He tried to act casual. "What about Schlipal?" But Aachen heard the fear in his voice.

"He's dead, you know?"

Even in the dim light, Aachen could see the colour drain from the butcher's face.

Aachen gripped the mop handle, ready in case Olster attacked him again. But the butcher didn't move.

"Did you kill him?" Aachen asked quietly. "Because he worked with the Canadian black market by pilfering his mess?"

Olster looked up and Aachen saw that his face was fearful, but also sad. He had never seen this man sad.

"Do you remember when we were peeling potatoes and you challenged me to find out why I was doing my KP at a different time than usual?" Aachen asked. "And I told you I was watching Schlipal to see if he was working with a Canadian civilian to deliver goods?"

Olster nodded slowly, his eyes blinking quickly.

"You called him a traitor and said you'd pay him a visit and make him answer for the pilfering." He paused, waiting for Olster to nod in response. The butcher only blinked but Aachen took that as affirmation for what he'd said. "So, did you do it?"

It took such a long time for Olster to move his head that it seemed barely perceptible. He nodded.

After another long moment, Olster spoke. His voice was not quite a whisper, but it was soft, a rare volume for the man. "I did it. This morning. Not sure why I waited, maybe because I was angry at Heidfeld and his goons for coming after me and I knew he was connected. But the chef was someone I could deal with. So I did. I went to his mess early this morning because I knew he would be there, told him what I thought of him, and he laughed at me. He said he wasn't involved with that shit anymore. Then he told me to fuck off and turned his back on me.

"I was going to leave but I changed my mind. I knew he was lying so I got him in a choke hold."

"And you killed him." Aachen sat up straight, looking for a better weapon than the mop. There was a bar used for weight-lifting. There were no weight plates on it but he knew it was a solid bar. But it was a few metres away. He wasn't sure if he would get there in time if Olster came at him.

But the man stayed put. "No," he said, shaking his head. "I didn't kill him. Almost, because he shit his pants. But like you, I let him go once he was unconscious. He was alive and breathing when I left him. Out cold, smelling of shit, but alive and breathing. I swear. I swear on the grave of my daughter and wife who were killed when my town was bombed last fall."

That gave Aachen pause. He hadn't known about the butcher's family, or their deaths. No wonder he was always angry. Olster was a soldier, a German soldier who had killed on the battlefield, but Aachen saw, in that moment, that the man was not a murderer.

After a moment, the corporal got up and left the butcher with his tears and grief in the wrestling room. He silently made a vow to do his best to protect Olster from Sergeant Heidfeld and his thugs.

12.

While Aachen was dealing with Sergeant Olster in the weight room, Neumann approached the hospital. A Canadian guard stood at the entrance, huddled in a thick fur coat to protect himself from the cold. He was large; bulky, but not fat. His chest was immense. He looked like a middle-aged Austrian farmer, hardened by generations of toil and living in high altitude.

When he spoke, the voice was deep, gravelly from decades of smoking cigarettes. "No entry," he said, surprisingly in German, with a hint of a Tyrolian accent. Somebody in this Canadian's family must have only left Austria recently.

Neumann introduced himself in German and explained why he should be allowed into the hospital, also in German, to test this guard's knowledge of the language.

"Right. You're the policeman in this place," the guard replied easily. "I've heard about you."

"Then you know I should be inside. I'm investigating this death."

"From what I hear, Major MacKay is investigating this death."

Neumann could have gone back and forth with the guard but instead just said, "If you tell Major MacKay that I'm outside, then I'm sure he'll want me inside."

The guard shrugged, then pounded on the door. It opened slightly and another Canadian appeared on the other side. "What's going on? This Kraut giving you a problem, Brunner?" he said in English.

The guard shook his head. "Got a sergeant by the name of Neumann," he replied, in English this time. "Asks if we could tell the major that he's outside."

"What are we, the fucking doormen?"

Brunner shrugged. "Just go tell the major, will ya?"

"All right, all right. Don't get your panties in a twist." The inside guard shut the door, leaving Neumann and Brunner alone outside. They stood in silence for a moment until Neumann reached into his pocket and pulled out a pack of cigarettes. He pulled the tip of one out and held the packet out to the guard.

Brunner pulled the cigarette out but instead of putting it in his mouth, he tucked it into his inside coat pocket. When he saw Neumann had pulled out his lighter, Brunner shrugged. "The major doesn't like us smoking on duty," he said in German.

"Ah, a stickler for the rules," Neumann said, cupping his hand to light his own cigarette. The smoke blew away quickly.

"The major is young," the Canadian said. "Disappointed to be missing the war."

"From what I've heard, he did have some battle experience. In Dieppe."

"Yeah, that was a total fuck-up." A pause. "But still, he wishes he could go back and fight." Brunner chuckled and shook his head.

"You don't wish you were fighting?" Neumann asked.

"Did my fighting in the Great One. That was enough for me."

"Where?" Neumann asked

"Vimy Ridge, Passchendaele, Mons, Amiens, Jigsaw Wood, Canal du Nord. All those terrible places."

"I was wounded in Amiens. Bullet through the arm. In and out, no infection. Barely feel it now."

"I got trench foot in Mons, stuck with me till the end. Almost lost a couple of toes. Cold like this always reminds me of it."

"Your German is good."

"Grandparents on both sides were born in Austria. Sort of passed on the language."

"They didn't mind you fighting for the Canadians?"

"They were all dead by then." Brunner's face got a faraway look. "Back in the trenches, because I could speak German, it was my job to yell at the other side during quiet moments, usually in the evenings. I was supposed to tell them to go home to their families instead of fighting. They kept telling me to go fuck my mother, things like that. So one day, I just started singing one of the folk songs my grandparents taught me, a bit of yodelling here and there, as best as I could, which wasn't very good."

Neumann chuckled.

"That's exactly the response I got from the other side. Laughter. Then one of them started too and his yodelling was much better than mine. Then a whole lot of them started singing and they yodelled for the rest of the night. It was quite a sound."

"I'm sure it was."

"Our boys thought it was a big laugh but our lieutenant didn't. He was some posh boy from Toronto and he didn't like that you guys were having a fun time because of what I'd started. I said 'Lieutenant, if they're singing songs like that all night, they're going to be homesick by tomorrow.' He didn't like that either, so the bastard said he was going to put me on report for aiding and abetting the enemy." The Canadian said nothing for a moment, a memory rising—probably a bad one. War was like that. "Sniper picked him off the next day, so nothing happened there."

The door to the hospital opened and the other soldier appeared again. "The major says this Kraut can come in. But only this one. No one else."

"You see anyone else out here?" Brunner said testily.

"Couple of Krauts by the sound of it." There was a joking tone to this Canadian's voice but there was a hint of nastiness to it.

"Just take Sergeant Neumann inside and fuck off, will you?"

"I only call it as I hear it," he said as he opened the door to let Neumann in.

The sergeant said nothing but before he walked into the hospital, he reached into his pocket, pulled out his pack of smokes, and handed it to Brunner. "Hope your foot gets better."

Brunner took the pack without question. "Don't let Hill bother you," he said, gesturing to the other guard as Neumann stepped through the threshold. "He's a bit of an asshole."

"Fuck you, Brunner."

Brunner ignored him and continued in English as if the other Canadian wasn't there. "Hill's problem is that he claims to have fought in the Great War but he never stepped foot on the battlefield, never lived in the trenches with the mud, blood, and rats like we did. He was still safe in jolly old England when the armistice was signed."

"Fuck you," said Hill. "Not my fault the war ended early. I still would have kicked any Kraut's ass if I got the chance."

"He don't know shit like we veterans do." Brunner said, slamming the door behind them.

The other guard, Hill, held a long cudgel, a large piece of oak with a huge knot at the end. Some of the Veterans Guards carried such clubs in the camp, leftovers from the time they served in the Great War. But unlike most of the other cudgels Neumann had seen, worn and weathered by age and use in battle decades before, this one was polished and smooth. It had never been used in battle.

Hill pointed it at Neumann. "If I faced you in the trenches, I would have smashed your head in, you fucking Nazi." He moved to poke Neumann in the shoulder with the bulbous end of the club. But the sergeant just batted it away and steeled his expression.

"Fuck you, Nazi prisoner. I'll teach you to disrespect us Canadians." He grinned and tapped the cudgel against the side of his leg, hitting a small leather holster to create a more dramatic sound.

Neumann stared for a moment at the holster, then, as Hill brought the cudgel up for a strike, he stepped inside the man's swing and grabbed the stick, pushing the guard back with his other hand. The guard stumbled backwards, allowing Neumann to yank the wooden weapon out of his grasp. When the guard regained his balance, Neumann held the cudgel for several seconds, tapping it against his leg the same way the Canadian had. He waited until the fury on the guard's face turned to fear. Then he tossed the heavy stick on the floor.

He stepped around the guard and moved down the hospital hallway towards the morgue. Behind him, he heard Hill scramble to pick up his cudgel and then follow behind, but Neumann walked as if he was unescorted.

13.

Neumann arrived at the door to the morgue and found a large Canadian standing in front of it. Both Neumann and the guard, a sergeant named Ford, recognized each other.

"Oh-ho! It's the great Sergeant Neumann. Hero of the Nazis," the guard drawled sarcastically.

"Greetings, Sergeant Ford. I hope all is well with you."

"There's another dead German so my day is made. A few more and you fuckers will have lost this war."

"Then we will no longer be enemies," Neumann said.

"But we'll never be friends," Ford said.

Hill, the other Canadian, laughed at that. But Sergeant Ford frowned, looking over Neumann's shoulder at the other guard. "Why are you still here, Hill? Get back to your fucking post."

The guard started to mutter something but thought better of it and slinked away.

"Fucking civilians," Ford grumbled. "Oh well. You'd better go in, Neumann. I'll have to search you though."

Neumann said nothing, just raised his arms above his head. Sergeant Ford roughly patted him down twice, once on the outside of his winter coat and again on the inside. "All right, let me take you in," Ford said when he was done.

He opened the door and ushered Neumann in with a bit of a push. Inside the room were four more people, if one did not count the corpse of Chef Schlipal. There was Corporal Knaup who stood in a corner, notebook in hand and rucksack placed at his feet. He had been scribbling but stopped to give Sergeant Neumann a nod.

There was also Dr. Kleinjeld, the chief medical officer for the camp. He stood near the examination table that held the chef's body. Kleinjeld seem perturbed, his face pinched.

The good doctor's annoyance was probably due to the two other people in the room. They were both Veterans Guards, although Major MacKay, who was standing next to the doctor, was much younger than the other Canadian; at maybe only twenty-five years old. Neumann had been interrogated by the Canadian major during the investigation into the death of Captain Mueller. Directly behind him was a much older and much larger Canadian, Sergeant Murray. Neumann also had dealings with Murray in the Mueller investigation.

It was the major who spoke when Neumann entered the room. His eyes lit up with delight. "Sergeant Neumann. I was wondering when you would join us."

The look on Sergeant Murray's face was not so welcoming.

He frowned deeply at Neumann's appearance in the morgue and stood up straight, like a boxer about to face an opponent, placing his right hand on the cudgel he had strapped to his belt.

Neumann snapped to attention and saluted the major. He saluted back and came around the table to greet Neumann, using a cane to assist the limp in his right leg. The sergeant remained at attention until the major came to stand directly in front of him.

"At ease, Sergeant Neumann," Major MacKay said, holding out his hand.

Neumann looked at the hand for a few seconds, and then extended his own. The major grabbed it and shook it vigorously. "It's good to see you again, Sergeant. Good to see you." Neumann nodded but did not reply.

The major turned and walked back to the examination table, beckoning Neumann to join him. Neumann followed. "I find it very interesting that you always seem to show up whenever there's a dead body in this camp," the major said, wagging a finger in the air.

"It's my job, sir," said Neumann. "I am the head of Civil Security and when an unfortunate situation like this occurs, I must investigate."

"Yes, I believe Murray called you the de facto chief of police for the Germans. And as the chief it is your duty to investigate such deaths, it seems."

"Yes sir. It is."

The major paused for a moment. "And how is the investigation going?" He gave Neumann a sideways glance.

"I have only begun."

"Oh, I'm sorry. I wasn't talking about Captain Schlipal here, although I'm sure your investigation will be thorough. I was talking about your other investigation." Neumann said nothing in response so the major continued, "Have you forgotten about Captain Mueller already, Sergeant Neumann? I heard you were injured while searching for his killer."

Neumann cleared his throat. "That investigation is … ongoing," he said plainly.

"Yes, I see." The major turned to face Neumann. "And General Horcoff's death? How's that investigation coming along?"

Corporal Knaup gasped slightly at the mention of the general. Major MacKay's eyes darted quickly in Knaup's direction, but the rest of his body remained still. He quickly turned his attention back to Neumann. The major had a slight, satisfied smirk on his face.

Neumann was impassive. "The general took his own life," he said without emotion.

"Yes, something to do with the attempt on Hitler's life, I believe," said the major. "But can you be sure of that? You were in the hospital so you were unable to conduct the investigation yourself."

"Of course."

"Quite a coincidence that you were injured at the same time as the general's death. Some might say it was too coincidental."

"I was injured during a sporting event."

"Yes, I heard that, too. Rugby, was it?" the major chuckled.

"You Germans certainly take your sports seriously for you to get so injured."

"We Germans believe that sports help build character."

"We Canadians believe the same thing," said the major, turning away from Neumann. "I've heard from Sergeant Murray here that some of the prisoners have really taken to hockey, that they play our game with a lot of spirit and that they've already established a league."

"I've heard that as well."

"Hockey is a fast and physical game so I hope Dr. Kleinjeld is prepared for some injuries during this season of yours."

"My staff and I shall endeavour to do our best if such injuries occur," the doctor said with distaste.

"Of course, of course," replied the major. "Despite the fact we are on opposite sides of a war, I have great faith in your medical abilities. Your work on Sergeant Neumann does you great credit. Less than four months ago he was in hospital with many broken bones, possibly some internal injuries, and here he is, standing next to me as if nothing happened."

"Sergeant Neumann can take as much of the credit for his recovery as I can," the doctor said. "He is a most resilient soldier. He is a prime example of German genetics at work."

"Yes, those German genetics are sure helping you guys in this war." Sergeant Murray laughed.

Major MacKay gave a Murray quick look of admonishment but quickly moved on. "Obviously, Captain Schlipal here was not a fine example of German genetics," he said. That drew a guffaw from Sergeant Murray.

"Captain Schlipal had his weaknesses," the doctor said. "Many who work in food service have similar weaknesses."

"I also hear that he had other not-so-positive attributes besides the more obvious physical ones," said MacKay.

"I am not sure of your meaning," Dr. Kleinjeld said.

"From what I hear, Captain Schlipal was not the most pleasant person to serve under."

"He was an asshole," Sergeant Murray added.

"I'm not sure why disparaging a deceased person's reputation has any relevance here," said the doctor with a disapproving tone.

"It has much relevance considering the manner of Captain Schlipal's death," MacKay said. "I'm sure Sergeant Neumann will agree with me."

Neumann said nothing.

The major turned to him. "Come Sergeant, you must have some opinions about Captain Schlipal's death and how it relates to his personality, how he interacted with people and some of his more … unsavoury dealings?"

Dr. Kleinjeld harrumphed but, again, Neumann did not respond.

"Even though Sergeant Neumann wishes to remain silent, I'm sure he's quite aware of Captain Schlipal's connections with black marketeers and how that might relate to his death." The sergeant was impassive. "Nothing to add, Sergeant?" the major asked, prodding further.

"If you wish to speculate on why Captain Schlipal was killed, then there is no need for me to stay," Dr. Kleinjeld said, pulling his pince-nez glasses from his pocket and placing them on his nose. "I have more important matters to attend to."

Sergeant Murray put a hand on the doctor's shoulder, which Kleinjeld attempted to shake off but Murray only gripped harder.

"Major, this type of behaviour is unbecoming," the doctor said. "If you wish for me to comment on the state of Captain Schlipal's body then get on with it. If not, then allow me to leave."

"Of course, of course, Dr. Kleinjeld," said the major, nodding to Sergeant Murray who released his hold on the doctor. MacKay gestured to Schlipal's body on the examination table. "Please, tell us what you've determined about the good chef's demise."

The major nudged Neumann with his cane. "Sergeant, please. If you have any comments, don't hesitate." Neumann again said nothing, but paid careful attention as the doctor pointed to the bruises on Schlipal's neck.

"These are obvious strangulation injuries that suggest a possible explanation for the Captain's death. Also, the enlargement of the tongue, the bursting of capillaries in the eyes and face, and the voiding of the bowels and bladder further indicate this possibility."

"So he was strangled to death?" asked Major MacKay.

"I cannot say for certain. I can only say it is highly possible," noted the doctor. "He was strangled, although I'm not sure if it was to the point of death. Probably to the point of unconsciousness, at least."

Neumann leaned in closer to look at the bruising on the

chef's neck. The bruises were more prevalent around the front of the neck, indicating that the Chef was attacked from behind. But he kept those thoughts to himself.

"What about these wounds on his chest?" asked the major, pointing at two stab wounds on the left side of Schlipal's torso. They were small but deep, and dried blood was caked around them.

"There is also one such wound on his back," added the doctor.

"Would these injuries have killed him?"

"The ones on his back and here in the stomach, probably not." answered Dr. Kleinjeld. He pointed to the wound in Schlipal's chest. "This one, though, is deep enough to have struck his heart."

"So that would have killed him."

"Definitely," said the doctor. "That was a mortal wound."

"And what could have caused such a wound?" the major asked. For a moment, no one responded.

"I might have an idea," Neumann said quietly.

Kleinjeld, Murray, and the major looked up from the body in surprise. After a moment, the major smiled. "Please, Sergeant Neumann, enlighten us."

Neumann turned away from the table and gestured for Corporal Knaup to bring the rucksack over. Knaup handed it to the sergeant. "I'm going to ask that what I am about to show to you stays in this room," Neumann said.

The smile on the major's face grew even wider. Neumann took a handkerchief from his pocket and wrapped it around his hand. He reached into the rucksack. "Please Major, this is not a joking matter. I've already ordered Corporal Knaup not to speak of it, and I'm sure Dr. Kleinjeld's oath of confidentiality will suffice for him. However, I need you to order your men to do as I asked. This doesn't leave the room."

"Okay, consider it done." MacKay pointed at Murray and then Ford. "Gentlemen, I'm directly ordering you not to speak of what you see in this room. Understand?"

Ford nodded, eyes wide. Murray grunted in disappointment, his mouth set in a deep frown.

"Do you understand, Sergeant Murray?"

He nodded but the frown remained in place.

"Okay Sergeant Neumann, I have agreed to your stipulations and I hope that you're not just leading us on. That what is in that bag will bear some light on this situation."

Neumann nodded. "It will. When I saw Captain Schlipal this morning, I pulled this from the body."

"Tampering with evidence is highly suspicious behaviour, Sergeant," said the major. "I thought you were a more professional investigator than that."

Neumann shrugged away the criticism. "I had my reasons, as I hope you'll see and understand."

"Just show us the damn thing," Murray barked with impatience.

Neumann pulled the kitchen towel from the bag. He set it on the examination table next to Schlipal's body, unwrapped its contents, and stepped back.

"Holy shit" said Sergeant Murray when he saw the short knife with the knuckle guard handle.

Kleinjeld's eyes went wide but he said nothing. Knaup looked at the ground while Ford tried to look over Neumann's shoulder to see the table. Major MacKay looked carefully at the knife, but seemed more taken by Murray's response. He turned towards him, eyes questioning.

Murray looked at him, his face pale. "That's a Robbins-Dudley Push Dagger," he said.

Major MacKay looked at the dagger again then up at Neumann. Neumann nodded. "This is not a German knife. It's British, and was standard-issue weaponry for Canadians who fought in the Great War."

14.

"Fuck me," groaned Sergeant Murray, giving Neumann a dirty look.

Major MacKay's mouth was set in a hard line. "Are you implying what I think you are, Neumann?" he asked in a clipped tone.

"I'm only pointing out the facts: this was the British push dagger that I found stuck in Captain Schlipal this morning," replied Neumann.

"You could've planted that knife," Murray snapped. He shouldered his way past Dr. Kleinjeld and rounded on Neumann on the other side of the table. Neumann turned, his hands clenched into fists at the side of his body. Knaup started forward as Sergeant Ford took a step towards the two men.

Major MacKay slammed his cane against the metal of the examination table, the crack of sound echoing through the room. "Sergeant Murray!" he shouted. "You will restrain yourself!"

Murray froze at the order, but he stared angrily at Neumann, poised to attack. Neumann was also ready to fight back.

"What reason would I have for planting a knife like this?" Neumann asked quietly.

"You're a fucking Kraut—that's enough for me," Murray hissed through his teeth.

"Sergeant Murray," the major said.

"Come on Major, you can't believe what this fucking Nazi is saying. You can't think that one of our boys killed this asshole on the table. Those Krauts have been killing each other ever since the war started."

"I'm not agreeing with him, Sergeant Murray, I'm just ordering you to control yourself."

Murray looked at Neumann for several more seconds, but then stepped back. His face and posture remained tense. "Fucking Nazi. You planted that knife, I know you did."

Neumann bristled at the other sergeant's name-calling. He wasn't a member of the National Socialist Party and he disagreed with many of their extremist policies, but he chose to say nothing to Murray's accusations. To the Canadians and other Allies, there was no distinction; all Germans were Nazis.

"He does have a point, Sergeant Neumann," MacKay said. "You show us this knife, one you say you took out of Captain Schlipal's body, but who can corroborate your story?"

"Corporal Knaup saw me take the knife out of the body," Neumann replied. Murray scoffed. "And there were many others in the mess who saw Captain Schlipal dead with this knife in his back."

"All fucking Nazis."

"I'll handle this, Sergeant Murray," the major warned. He turned back to Neumann. "Again, Sergeant Murray has a valid point. Only German prisoners will say they saw a knife in Schlipal. What's to say they aren't just supporting a lie of one of their own?"

"I think the question you should be asking, Major MacKay, is why was there a British dagger sticking out of Captain Schlipal?"

"So you claim. But why should we believe anything you, an enemy prisoner, says? I cannot trust you."

"I cannot trust you either, but still I showed you the knife."

"And why did you do that? To suggest that a Canadian may be involved in Schlipal's death."

"And why is that so terrible to imagine? You said so yourself that Schlipal was involved in unsavoury dealings with the black market, smuggling food and supplies from his mess out of the camp. And who can get those things out of the camp? A German prisoner? Of course not. Only a Canadian could have helped Schlipal move his black market goods out of this camp. Maybe not one of your men, Major, but still a Canadian."

MacKay considered this thought for a while. "Just because Schlipal may have had dealings with some of the guards doesn't mean he was killed by one of them. This knife is meaningless because we can't prove it's entirely connected to Schlipal based on your word alone."

"I'm sure Dr. Kleinjeld could help with that," Neumann said.

Kleinjeld stepped forward and, without touching it, looked more closely at the knife. "The size and shape of the blade does correspond to the size and shape of the stab wounds," he said. "Although there's no way for me to confirm that this was the actual dagger that caused the wounds."

"See? Even your own German doctor can't confirm this knife is connected to Schlipal," MacKay said. "By removing it from his body, as you claim you did, you actually destroyed any evidence to support your theory that Canadians were involved."

Murray laughed at that. Major MacKay shot him a quick look but the Canadian sergeant ignored it.

"I had my reasons for removing it," Neumann said quietly.

"And those reasons were?" the major asked.

Neumann sighed and looked around the room. He glanced at the knife, at Schlipal, and wondered if he did make a mistake by removing the weapon from the body. But he looked at dagger again and realized he had not. "As soon as I saw that dagger sticking out of Schlipal, I knew what it was. I fought too many hand-to-hand battles against men like Sergeants Murray and Ford in the Great War to not recognize that dagger. And when I was captured in that war, it was that kind of dagger that I stole from a British soldier and used to escape."

"You used it to kill him. And others," MacKay said, his eyes narrowing.

"Yes I did. It was war and they were the enemy. That's the nature of war; kill or be killed."

"I should kill you right now," Murray said.

"You could try," Neumann said flatly. "But I would get to that dagger and slit Major MacKay's throat before you even got close. Then I would come after you."

MacKay balked and slowly reached for the dagger, grasping it firmly as he took a step away from Neumann.

"Although I would not do so unless I was attacked," reassured Neumann.

"It's probably your knife, isn't it?" Murray said, reaching for his cudgel.

Neumann laughed. "Yes, Sergeant Murray," he scoffed. "I killed those British lads on the battlefield in 1917 and kept it as a souvenir. Then I brought it with me to this war, through all the battles I fought in Poland, France, North Africa. And when I was taken prisoner, stripped off all my clothes, searched through every orifice in my body, I managed to smuggle it here just so I could plant it on a dead chef."

"There's no need to be sarcastic, Sergeant Neumann," the major said. "You still haven't explained why you removed the dagger from Schlipal, as you claim you did."

"I did remove it, and I'll tell you why. As I said, I recognized that dagger as soon as I saw it. And there are many Germans in this camp who would recognize it too. We Germans understand the importance of using veteran experience; we don't keep experienced soldiers like Sergeants Murray and Ford here, or Sergeant Brunner outside, on the home front to guard prisoners. We don't waste their knowledge, their patriotism for their country. We would have them on the front lines, using their wisdom to help fight the enemy directly.

"You have hundreds of these veterans in your camp who would have known that dagger on sight. Word would have spread quickly that Chef Schlipal was killed by a Canadian. No one would care if he was an asshole, a thief, and a black marketeer. All they would see is a German killed by a Canadian and you would have been facing a camp of 12,000 angry prisoners. It would be a bloodbath. So I took the knife to prevent that violence. To prevent any more Germans from being killed by Canadian soldiers."

15.

By the time he got back to his hut, Aachen was exhausted. And not the good kind of exhaustion after a day of wrestling matches. It was like the exhaustion he felt after countless days of endless combat, his body screaming in pain and hunger, his muscles groaning, his legs barely able to hold him up, let alone walk the rest of the way to his bunk. But this exhaustion was also different; there was no tension in his body, no alertness or adrenaline that would give him a quick boost of energy if something unexpected was to occur.

Aachen knew that if he was in combat and there was an ambush or an artillery barrage, he would not have the strength to protect himself, to fight back, or to dive into a hole to escape the bullets and shrapnel.

But in a strange way, he hoped for something like death. Because death would be rest and Aachen wanted nothing more than to lie down on his bunk and sleep until the end of the war.

He trudged along the lines of double bunks in the hut. He arrived at the one he shared with Sergeant Neumann and sighed with disappointment when he realized he would have to find some strength to climb up to the top bunk. He looked at it for several seconds and then decided to just sit down on the sergeant's for a moment to catch his breath.

A few minutes later, Aachen decided that he if only just laid down on the sergeant's bunk, he could rest easier for a second or two. He was awoken sometime later by Neumann's voice. "Comfortable, Corporal Aachen?"

Aachen woke quickly and took in the scene in front of him: Neumann was sitting on the foot of his bunk, an amused look on his face and Knaup was standing, leaning with his left shoulder on the neighbouring bunk, smoking a cigarette, sporting a big grin.

"My apologies, Sergeant. I must have fallen asleep," Aachen croaked. His throat hurt with each syllable. He tried to sit up but the quick movement caused his head to spin. He fell back on the bunk and closed his eyes for a moment to stop the world from spinning. When he opened them again, the room was still, but the exhaustion he felt weighed him down.

He tried to get up again, but the sergeant put one of his large hands on Aachen's chest and easily pushed him down. Aachen had no strength to resist. "You look horrible, Corporal, so I'm ordering you to stay in my bunk until you look less shitty."

"But Sergeant—" Aachen started to say, but the sound

caught in his sore throat. He had to clear it several times but it still hurt.

"What happened to your voice?" Knaup asked, blowing a large cloud of smoke. "You sound like my grandfather after a full day in the mines."

"Olster," Aachen managed to croak but that was all he could get out.

"Put out your damn cigarette, Knaup," Neumann barked, "and go get Aachen some water."

Knaup stiffened and almost saluted with the cigarette in his hand. He put it out on the side of the neighbouring bunk, adding another burn mark to the several that were already there. "Sorry, Aachen," Knaup stammered. "I'll go get some water." He grabbed the canteen hanging off the end of Neumann and Aachen's bunks and dashed towards the washroom.

When he was out of earshot, Neumann moved in closer to Aachen. "So, you found Olster?" he asked. Aachen started to speak but the words wouldn't come out. Neumann waved a hand. "Don't try to speak. It's obvious, not just by your voice but by the bruises on your throat that you've been injured. Was it Olster?"

Aachen nodded, his face flushing at the same time.

"There's no need to beat yourself up about it, Aachen. He probably caught you by surprise and because of our injuries this summer, our bodies are not as strong as they used to be."

Aachen closed his eyes and sighed. The sergeant was right. Aachen felt vulnerable, a feeling he had rarely felt in his life. He had always been strong, especially physically. But to be so weak that he could not push himself up from the sergeant's bed was embarrassing, to say the least.

"It's not easy, is it?" Neumann said, as if reading Aachen's mind.

Aachen nodded and Neumann smiled slightly, laying a hand on the young man's chest in an affectionate gesture. "Did Olster kill Schlipal?"

Aachen paused, then shook his head.

"Are you sure?" Neumann asked.

Aachen nodded. But to ensure the sergeant believed him, he spoke, even though it hurt. "He didn't do it."

Neumann looked at him for a moment. Aachen started to speak again but the sergeant waved at him to stop. "Don't speak, Corporal. I believe you. You can tell me your reasons later, when you're in better shape to do so. Also, after our visit to the hospital and talking to Dr. Kleinjeld, I'm inclined to agree with your assessment."

Aachen raised an eyebrow, signalling for the sergeant to continue.

Neumann filled him in on what happened at the hospital. Knaup returned halfway through the retelling and silently handed Aachen the canteen. The corporal pushed himself into a slightly more elevated position and drank slowly. The water was cool, refreshing. That was one of the best things about being in Canada; water that was clean and clear, nothing like the brackish, dirty water in North Africa, even better than the water back home. He drank deeply and Neumann handed him a bread roll, one that he had pocketed from the bakers' hut.

Aachen took a bite of the fresh roll and smiled as he felt his energy returning.

When Neumann got to the part where he revealed the knife to the Canadians, Aachen shook his head. "A bit dramatic, don't you think?" The food and water had soothed his throat somewhat.

Neumann shrugged. "I had a point to make to the Canadians."

"Do you … believe … one of them killed …" Aachen rasped.

Neumann shrugged. "Despite what Sergeant Murray thought, there's no way a German could have managed to smuggle it in here." He gestured to Aachen as the corporal finished the last of the bread roll. "And in all the time we served together, Aachen, did you ever see me with a dagger from the Great War?"

"Not the type … for souvenirs," Aachen replied.

"Souvenirs only weigh you down," Neumann said. "And not just in battle. Once you're home, the medals and trinkets only keep you in the past. You boys remember that. Life goes on after war and you've got to move on with it.

Knaup and Aachen exchanged a solemn look.

"But returning to problem at hand," Neumann continued, "if the dagger wasn't brought in by a prisoner, it had to come from the outside. A Canadian, or someone working with the Canadians, must have killed Schlipal.

"I have … a suggestion," Aachen said. He drank another gulp of water.

"And I agree with that suggestion. But we both know

Heidfeld isn't the kind to do his own dirty work. If he was involved, he would have gotten someone else to do it." Neumann pushed himself up from the bunk and sat on the neighbouring one to face Aachen.

"But before we even approach Heidfeld, we need information. Our baker Beck clearly suggested that pilfering in Mess #3 was on the rise, comparable to when I had a talk with Schlipal last summer. What we have to do is go to the administration building and check the numbers to see if it has, in fact, increased."

"And if—"

Neumann held a hand up to stop Aachen from straining his voice further. "I know, Corporal, I know. If the pilfering is up, someone in administration has to have noticed it. And last time this happened, we were notified and sent to deal with Chef Schlipal. So why are they withholding information from us now?"

16.

The camp administration was housed in what was originally supposed to be a classroom building. It was commandeered by the command of the camp when the Canadians refused to construct an admin building, arguing that there were already enough buildings in the camp. So they worked with what was available. The second-most eastern classroom building was where Neumann and Knaup headed.

Aachen wanted to come with them, but Neumann ordered him to stay put and get some rest. He knew the corporal was feeling guilty about not helping, but he had done enough so far and been injured in the process. Neumann even told Aachen that he could use his bunk instead of climbing up into his own.

The sergeant figured he might drop in on Olster to see how the butcher was doing, to make sure no one had found him and did him any harm. Neumann didn't like Olster—not many did—but he respected the butcher. He had been brutal on his squad in battle, but unlike some tough commanders, Olster didn't shirk his duty, didn't stay in the rear when his squad was in the fight. He fought side by side with his men, screaming and slapping them forward. He was a true front-line soldier.

Like many front-line soldiers, Neumann felt no love for administrators. He understood their necessity in war; someone had to make sure equipment and supplies got sorted and sent to the proper destinations, that orders were copied, checked, double-checked, and copied again to ensure there wasn't a breakdown in communication. And in the camp, they were responsible for housing, feeding, and organizing thousands of prisoners in the wilds of Canada.

But he didn't like how some administrators, who had never set foot on a battlefield, claimed that their job was more important than any other. That the men who fought and died in battle were just numbers on sheets of paper or plastic pieces on maps that could to be pushed around and the war would be won.

Which is why Neumann was annoyed when the clerk refused to give him the requisition and usage figures for Schlipal's kitchen.

"What do you mean 'unavailable'?" Neumann asked, stepping up to the desk. He leaned forward to tower over the young private. The man, named Rier, did his best to stare back at the sergeant through his cracked wire-rimmed glasses, but was unable to hold the gaze.

"I'm s-s-sorry, Sergeant," Rier stammered. He pulled his

glasses off and made to clean them with his handkerchief as a means to look away and hide his fear of Neumann. The hand holding the glasses shook slightly. "The information you request is unavailable at this time."

"Just 'unavailable,' or unavailable to me?"

"Unavailable," Rier said, quickly glancing up at Neumann before returning to cleaning his glasses. "Sorry Sergeant. There's really nothing I can do," he whispered so that only Neumann could hear and gave him a pleading look.

Neumann leaned back. "But as the head of Civil Security, I have the right to see those forms. It was you, Rier, who brought it to my attention when there was a discrepancy between the supplies that Schlipal had been given and what was being used. I was allowed to see those papers before, so why can't you give them to me now?"

Rier looked up at Neumann and shrugged without saying anything.

"Because I ordered him not to," said a voice behind them.

Rier glanced around Neumann. He jumped to his feet and snapped to attention, dropping his glasses onto his desk, cracking them even further. Knaup instinctively mirrored the private's reaction, without knowing who had just entered the room.

Neumann turned to see and he snapped to attention as well, saluting in the Wehrmacht way. A lieutenant in a perfectly pressed Wehrmacht uniform had entered the room. Neumann stared at the man and immediately recognized him. He knew that this lieutenant was a member of the Waffen

SS, the highest-ranking SS officer in the camp. He only wore the Wehrmacht uniform because the Canadians had forbidden any display of Nazi symbols, including the wearing of SS uniforms.

The lieutenant brought his arm up, palm forward. "Heil Hitler," he said. A second later, Knaup and Rier both stuck their right arms out at a forty-five degree angle. "Heil Hitler!" they shouted.

Neumann returned the salute, but in a more casual manner. "Heil Hitler," he said quietly. He did not relax from standing at attention.

For some, like Knaup and Rier, the lieutenant was someone to be feared. For Neumann, he was someone to move cautiously around, like a tied up dog with a history of breaking free of his collar.

The lieutenant was thin, but not skinny, and when he approached them from across the room, he carried himself upright with perfect posture. He also spoke with perfect, high-German enunciation.

"I am the one who gave the order which Private Rier speaks of," the SS lieutenant said as he stopped in front of Neumann. He stared at the sergeant, but Neumann did not make eye contact. One never did with a dog that could attack at any moment.

But that didn't stop him from speaking. "I have been given the right in the past to view administrative documentation that pertains to my ongoing investigations. It's in the manifest of my duty and obligations as the head of Civil Security."

"Your privileges have been changed," the lieutenant replied. The tone of his voice suggested that that was the final word.

"Why?" Neumann asked. "Sir," he added, after a moment.

The lieutenant stepped back slightly, surprised by the question. "There is no need to know why, just that things have changed. This order was passed on to you, and you must accept it."

"Of course, Lieutenant," Neumann, nodded. He paused. "However, I only ask to ensure that I fully understand what has been changed in my manifest." This time Neumann did make eye contact and held it. "As a loyal and decorated member of the Wehrmacht and the Fatherland in this war and the previous one, I don't wish to become derelict in my duty … sir."

The lieutenant smiled but there was nothing pleasant about it. "Your contribution to the Fatherland is well noted, Sergeant Neumann. As is your loyalty and dedication. But times are changing and with these changing times, we must adjust."

"But I am investigating the recent death of Captain Schlipal and that information I request would—"

"The information is not available to you!" the lieutenant snapped, his face turning red.

Neumann stiffened and quickly turned his gaze away. "Yes, Lieutenant."

The lieutenant, who was almost as tall as the sergeant, stepped up to Neumann so that his face was only inches away. His eyes were bloodshot, his skin blotchy, and his breath smelled of cigarettes and cabbage. "You will not bother Private Rier or anyone else in this building for this information, do you understand? If you continue to do so, you will be relieved from your post as head of Civil Security and all the protections that gives you." The lieutenant breathed heavily on Neumann. "Do you understand that, Sergeant? Do you understand what that means?"

Neumann nodded. "Yes, Lieutenant."

The SS officer leaned in for a few more seconds to make a point, then backed away. "Good, then we are all on the same page. As you were," he said, making to leave the room. As he got to the door, Neumann, still standing at attention, called out to him.

"Should I continue investigating Captain Schlipal's death then, Lieutenant?" The officer stopped in mid-step and started to turn. Neumann added, "If you have any information you wish to give about his death, it would make it easier for me to do my duty."

The lieutenant's face was flaming red. He breathed loudly through his nose. Still, he held his anger in check, although only barely, speaking through tight lips. "I do not understand what you are talking about, Sergeant. Are you intimating something? Because that would be very unwise."

"No, Lieutenant, I'm not intimating anything. I am only asking if there was any official involvement in Captain Schlipal's death. In the same way there was with General Horcoff's because of his traitorous connection to those who attempted to assassinate the Führer. Because if there was, as was the case with the General, then I would not need to investigate further."

The lieutenant looked at Neumann, trying to see if there

was falseness in his voice. But Neumann held his own. His question was an honest one. He needed to know if someone in the command section ordered Schlipal killed, possibly for resuming his pilfering again. Stealing from the Fatherland, even in a prisoner-of-war camp, in addition to working with the enemy through the Canadian black market, was punishable by death. Schlipal was a known offender and had been issued a warning before, but it was possible that he was punished for failing to comply with these orders. Or for some other reason. If so, then Neumann would not investigate further, no matter how he felt about it.

"There was nothing official about the death of Schlipal," said the lieutenant. "However, I must warn you to tread carefully on this, Sergeant Neumann. I've heard what you told the Canadians and that distresses me. And do not bother anyone in this building again with requests like the one you made today."

"Of course, Lieutenant." He saluted. "Heil Hitler."

The officer was caught off guard by the salute but recovered quickly. He snapped his right arm up, shouting the salute. Knaup and Rier did the same. And as quickly as he had entered the room, the SS lieutenant was gone.

A second later, Knaup and Rier let out deep sighs of relief. Rier fell back into his chair, reaching for his glasses. "Jesus, Neumann. You are a crazy fucker."

"Sorry, Rier," Neumann said with a shrug. "I had no idea the situation had changed like this. I won't bother you again with requests about this and any other papers. And as the head of

Civil Security, I would strongly suggest you keep those papers locked up for the next day or so. Just to be safe. You never know who may be coming around now that official channels are closed."

Rier blinked at Neumann several times. They stared at each other for a few moments until Rier shook his head in incredulity. He dramatically waved for Neumann and Knaup to leave. "Get the fuck out of here, Neumann, and let me get back to work!" He shouted loudly enough to ensure that almost everyone in the building heard the exchange. "Leave me in peace."

Neumann nodded and motioned for Knaup to follow him. "Let's get the fuck out of here, Corporal, before we get into any more trouble."

17.

A few hours later, Neumann was in his mess, eating lunch. Knaup and Aachen were seated with him at his regular table, tucked near a corner behind a large wooden beam for a bit of privacy. Aachen was looking a bit better after a few good hours of sleep and he ate heartily, slicing big chunks of Hackbraten—a meatloaf dish with boiled eggs cooked inside—onto slices of bread slathered with butter. There were mashed potatoes too and Aachen had a large pile in his bowl, also drowned in butter.

Neumann and Knaup ate more slowly, but Neumann was glad to see Aachen eating well. It meant that the corporal was on the mend, despite the attack by Olster that morning.

While Aachen ate, Neumann, with some side comments from Knaup, filled the corporal in with what transpired in the administration building.

Aachen was surprised and disappointed in the situation but he waited to speak until after he had finished eating, punctuating his meal with a large glass of milk. He belched and wiped his face. "That's not a good development, the Waffen SS playing a role in this. Are you sure that he was being truthful when he said Schlipal's death was not an official one?"

Neumann nodded. "I'm very sure he was telling the truth. Schlipal's death was not official but that doesn't mean the Waffen SS isn't involved somehow. Or maybe it's just the good lieutenant that's involved, but in a non-official capacity."

"You really think he'd do something like that?"

Neumann shrugged as he chewed his meatloaf. "It's very possible, especially now. With the end of the war in sight and the Fatherland on the losing end again, those who once held power outside of Berlin are losing their authority. No doubt the farther you get from Berlin, the less power you have now. The SS and others may be looking for another way to re-establish their authority, or to at least hold on to what's left."

Aachen considered that. "So he could be looking for someone whose power has recently increased in the camp."

"Heidfeld," Knaup said quickly. When he saw how fast the other two reacted to the interruption, his face turned red. "Sorry."

"Don't be sorry, Knaup," said Neumann. "You're absolutely correct."

Aachen nodded and punched Knaup playfully on the arm. "See? He's starting to rub off on you," he said, nodding towards the sergeant. "But don't worry, it's not a deadly contagion, only a nuisance, like a bad cold."

Neumann tried to ignore the comment but couldn't help but smile slightly. The offhand jibe at a superior soldier, especially within earshot, meant Aachen was feeling much better. Neumann forced a stern look and continued with his commentary as if nothing had been said.

"It is highly probable that the SS lieutenant is connected to Heidfeld. It's a smart move for both of them. Heidfeld can use his connections with the SS to intimidate the other prisoners, while the SS gain some semblance of authority by aligning themselves with Heidfeld and his growing influence. It's important now since the war may end soon. The SS are going to need all the help they can get to make it through the aftermath because they'll have to answer for their actions, many of which were criminal."

Knaup couldn't help but gasp when he heard Neumann's statement. Even Aachen paused, his refilled glass of milk halfway to his lips. But he also nodded. "When I was in the hospital I overheard one of the nurses treating an SS corporal for a nasty burn on his underarm. The doctor asked how and why he got such a burn but the corporal just told him to shut up and bandage him up."

"Smart corporal," Neumann said. "But I'm not too sure about the lieutenant. Heidfeld isn't someone to trust. If his needs require it, he'll turn on that lieutenant without a second thought."

"It'll be the same for the SS. Heidfeld is walking a fine line by allying himself with them; that is, if that's really what's going on."

"It's quite obvious he is," Knaup said. He didn't flush or apologize for speaking out of turn this time. "The black market is Heidfeld's operation, everyone in the camp knows that. If you want contraband, you talk to Heidfeld or one of his men. And you said so yourself earlier that when you told Captain Schlipal to cease pilfering last summer, it was Heidfeld who got upset. And since the lieutenant is denying you access to all paperwork related to how mess supplies are doled out and implemented, sergeant, then it follows that they must show that pilfering has increased. He's locking down the documents to protect his, or someone else's, interests."

Neumann and Aachen looked at each other and smiled as Knaup spoke. A look of quiet disappointment came over Knaup's face. "For an SS officer, the lieutenant's not very subtle," he said.

"Neither is Heidfeld with his overt threats against Sergeant Olster," Aachen said.

"Heidfeld has never been subtle. He's a criminal and he wants everyone to know it," Neumann said. "He thinks it gives him more power, thinks if he broadcasts all that he does, he's instilling fear in everyone."

"Many are afraid of him," Knaup noted.

"And that's smart because Heidfeld is a dangerous man," Neumann said. "But in my experience, smart criminals don't talk that much. Criminals who are always boasting about their operations and how powerful and dangerous they are invite not only visits and prosecution from law enforcement, but also mistrust from other criminals who wish to remain more circumspect. And in the crime business, it's always best to have the other criminals on your side. Or to at least have them trust you."

"How can criminals trust each other?" Knaup asked. "They're criminals."

Neumann started to explain but Aachen cut him off. He didn't want the conversation to get off track. "It's too bad we can't get any of that information from administration."

"Nobody else in the camp has access to that information," Knaup said. "And even if they did, what good would it do? Not only do we have Heidfeld and a member of command involved in it, but based on the dagger we found in Schlipal's body, a Veterans Guard or two might also be involved."

"It could give us a clue about what happened to Schlipal," Aachen said. "And I think that's probably the important thing here."

Knaup nodded and the two corporals turned to the sergeant. He had a thoughtful look on his face. "I've been thinking about that," he said quietly. "And I might have an idea." He pointed at Aachen. "How are you feeling, Klaus? Are you up for a bit of exercise this evening?"

"The fresh air will do me good," Aachen said with a large grin.

"Are you sure?" Neumann asked. "I want you to be honest with me. Don't be too proud to admit if you're not ready. You won't help me if you're not."

"I'm ready," Aachen said confidently.

"Good," Neumann said with a nod. He turned to Knaup.

"Where are we going tonight?" Knaup asked quickly, his voice rising in pitch. He was like a little boy heading off on his first outdoor camping trip.

"Tonight, you're going nowhere, Dieter," Neumann said. The corporal's face fell slightly but he recovered quickly, accepting the order. "I need you to find someone on the Escape Committee, doesn't matter who; they are all trustworthy men. Tell them that I sent you and tell them I need the maps to all the tunnels they've dug in the camp and bring them to me."

Knaup started to ask why but held back. He nodded. "Yes Sergeant."

"Also, tell them to clear the decks tonight. Whoever you talk to will understand."

"I don't think anybody's planning an escape this late in the war," Aachen said. "Or at this time of year. They'll miss the Christmas celebrations."

"No matter, I don't want anyone mucking about tonight." Neumann pointed again to Knaup. "You've got your orders, Corporal."

"Yes Sergeant," replied Knaup.

"Good. Then get going."

18.

The Canadians did a count in the late afternoon, just before the sun went down. They took their time doing so, keeping the prisoners standing in the cold for more than two hours. They even pulled a few out of the lines and searched them. At the same time, a good number of guards went into the barracks while the prisoners stood in formation for the count.

Neumann knew that this was all his fault, that handing them the dagger and implying a guard might be involved in Schlipal's death made the Canadians want to see if there were any other weapons in the barracks. But this was also a show of power, to demonstrate that the Canadians were in full control of the camp and that there were no lapses in security, even though the war was expected to end soon.

The prisoners grumbled and complained, calling the Veterans Guards every terrible name one could say in German.

But at least no one physically disrupted the count by moving around as the Canadians did their calculations, or by giving false names and hut locations. It was too cold for those kinds of shenanigans.

Once the count was over, Neumann and Aachen went to the mess to eat. Knaup joined them and quietly handed over the map from the Escape Committee. Neumann and Aachen examined it carefully as they ate before returning it to Knaup, who tucked it into his rucksack.

After dinner, Neumann and Aachen helped with KP and walked back to their hut for the nightly lockdown, the time when all prisoners had to be in their barracks. But they did not go to their bunks. Instead, they headed to the latrines, near the centre of the hut.

The latrine area was divided into three main sections. The first was the actual latrine section which had a large number of toilets in an open space without walls. Most of the prisoners only used this area for defecation; if they needed to urinate, they usually just stepped outside. The second area was for washing, which had the same number of metal sinks as there were toilets. And then there was the showering section which, like the toilets, was open and communal. There were several rows of showers separated by walls of concrete that did not reach the ceiling and showerheads extended from the pipes that ran along them. Each shower had a wooden pallet for prisoners to stand on to prevent the spread of foot fungus.

Each of the three latrine areas was occupied by a handful of prisoners, but most just went on with their daily self-care activities and paid little attention to Neumann and Aachen. Despite the openness of the area, most of the prisoners tried their best to give each other privacy and kept their eyes to themselves.

At the back of the latrine, there was also a utility room tucked behind the showers. This room held the hot water tanks as well as the cleaning supplies for the space. The hut's upkeep was the responsibility of the prisoners so every man was part of a cleaning rotation, save for people with other duties, like Neumann and Aachen.

The utility room door was normally locked with only a few people possessing keys, such as the Hut Leader and the Barracks Warden and their assistants. Neumann also had a key for this room, as well as for many similar utility rooms throughout the camp. Prisoners were very creative in finding hiding spaces for the illicit activities they wanted to keep away from Neumann, such as making illegal alcohol or gambling. They also used the spaces to plan escapes, and to use and store shortwave radios away from the watchful eyes of the Canadians.

Neumann saw light under the door, which told him that the room was being used. Instead of unlocking the door and surprising whoever was in there, he knocked lightly, using a simple code pattern.

He heard shuffling inside the room, a tip-toeing of footsteps, and the sound of the door being unlocked. It opened slightly. Cautiously peeking through was the face of a captain named Simons who had been in the same battalion in North Africa with Neumann and Aachen. Simons had a receding hairline of dirty-blond hair and a small yet bushy walrus moustache. His brown, bloodshot eyes looked over a pair of wire-rimmed reading glasses that were perched on the end of his narrow nose. Although he was older than the average soldier, he was probably only in his mid-30s, not old enough to have served in the Great War.

A look of relief washed over Simons' face when he saw Neumann. "Oh thank God, it's only you," Simons said in a whisper. "I'm a bit busy in here so if you need anything, make it quick."

"We're just passing through, Captain Simons. Aachen and I won't bother you."

Simons' gave a quick look behind him, then turned back. He nodded. "Of course. I won't get in your way." He opened the door wider and gestured for them to come in. He shut the door behind them quickly and locked it before squeezing past the two larger men to an area behind the hot water tanks.

Neumann followed slowly behind him, while Aachen started to dissemble a tower of boxes containing bleach and cleaning fluid by moving them away from the wall they were stacked along to the opposite side of the room. He moved slowly, lifting only one box at a time so as not to injure himself in the process.

Neumann found Simons sitting on a small stool next to a tiny square table. On it was a bric-a-brac metal contraption that seemed to have been haphazardly created from random pieces of debris found in the camp. Pieces of flattened tin had been roughly welded together to create an oddly-shaped box with just two high sides and a bottom. One side of the box had two knobs; one made from the round top of a metal coffee thermos, and the other was a small bit of wood. The other welded plate had a large, thicker circular knob that had once been half of a food can, now stuffed with wool and covered with a cloth. Inside the box was half the body of a flashlight, what looked to be remnants of a lighting fixture sitting on top of it, and a square battery; Neumann had no idea where Simons got the latter. Wires, cords, and string were laced throughout the entire artifact.

It looked like an abstract sculpture Neumann might have seen in a museum in Frankfurt between the wars. But even though Neumann didn't understand the mechanics of the piece, he knew it had more practical applications. It was actually a powerful shortwave radio receiver built from stolen supplies, and only one of many scattered throughout the camp.

Static was emanating from the giant tin can filled with wool as Simons moved the larger knob on the side back and forth. Neumann did not know all the specifics of operating a shortwave radio, but knew the German government had plenty of stations spreading news of the war. Some broadcasts were obvious and with stable frequencies while others were more clandestine and with continually changing frequencies.

The Canadians called it "Nazi propaganda," but for many of the prisoners, this was the most reliable source of news from the homefront. The Canadians knew that the radios existed and spent a good amount of manpower to find and then destroy them. In the past month, however, they had lessened their search efforts because even the German stations couldn't hide the fact that the Allies were winning. Neumann wondered if they would intensify their searches as retaliation for what had happened earlier today in the hospital. A more strict count in the afternoon showed they were, but that could turn out to be a short-lived reaction.

"Any news?" Neumann asked.

Simons moved the larger knob on the side back and forth with his left hand while holding a pencil over a notepad with his right. All they could hear was static.

Simons shook his head. "It's very quiet tonight," he said without turning around. "It's been very quiet for a few days now. A bit of basic news, some opera here and there, but nothing of value."

"Maybe the silence is what's important," Neumann said.

"That's always a possibility," Simons replied with a nod. "Radio silence is usually standard protocol before an attack."

"You believe there'll be a push soon?" Neumann looked over to see how Aachen was progressing. The corporal was moving slowly, but seemed able to handle the boxes. The floor underneath them would soon be exposed.

"We've been expecting one for weeks, which is why somebody is here at all times."

"You get the short straw and the night shift?"

"Night shift is the best time for this because Europe is eight hours ahead of us. If something happens at dawn or during the day, I'm one of the first to hear about it."

"Always good to be the first to hear news, isn't it?"

"Sometimes, but it all depends on whether it's good or bad." The static cleared for a moment and was replaced by the sound of semi-regular beeps. Both Neumann and Simons leaned closer to the radio speaker to better hear the Morse code, and Simons scribbled letters on his pad without looking. Even Aachen stopped mid-lift to listen. Neumann picked up a few letters here and there but his Morse code had become rusty since he was captured.

After a tense couple of moments, Simons relaxed and stopped writing. "Only some kind of merchant shipping signal, probably on the west coast. Nothing of value." Neumann's shoulders dropped in disappointment, while Aachen shrugged and continued moving the boxes. Simons turned the knob away from the Morse signals and the static returned.

"Sergeant," Aachen said.

Neumann turned to see the newly cleared space on the floor. He put a hand on Simons' shoulder. "We'll leave you to it, Captain."

"Travel well," Simons said. "I'll close up when you leave."

Neumann stepped over to where Aachen was crouching. The corporal had already pried one of the floorboards away and was working on the others.

Because the Canadians hadn't had the time to dig foundations for any of the buildings when they were hastily constructing the camp, they had used concrete piles buried into the ground to support the structures. As a result, all of the buildings in the camp had a one-and-a-half-metre crawl space underneath them.

For the most part, the prisoners used these spaces to hide their tunnel-digging efforts. This was why a group of Veterans Guards, nicknamed The Gophers, routinely inspected these areas and then filled in or collapsed the tunnels.

The prisoners also had other uses for the crawl spaces.

There were one, sometimes two, secret entrances to the crawl space in each hut or building, depending on its size. They were usually hidden underneath a pile of boxes in a utility room, as was the case in Neumann's hut, or under an unused bunk. Once in the crawl space, one could move to the perimeter of the building to find two or three concealed entrances that led outside.

None of these access points were marked in any way, not even secretly, which is why Neumann needed the map from the Escape Committee. In addition to mapping all the tunnels in the camp, it also plotted the hidden entrances for every building.

From the outside access points, one could quickly run to the next building, find a hidden entrance, and gain entry into the crawl space. From there, you could enter that hut if the way was clear, or traverse underneath it and repeat the process to gain access to the next neighbouring building.

In this way, prisoners could travel between huts, or across the entire camp at night without the Canadians noticing.

Once he removed the second floor panel, Aachen dropped down to the ground underneath the barracks. He crawled away from the opening and disappeared into the dark. Neumann slipped his gloves on and climbed in after him.

19.

As soon as Sergeant Neumann hit the ground underneath the hut, he regretted this plan. For a man who was almost two metres tall, even crawling on his hands and knees barely gave Neumann enough clearance. It was slow going for the sergeant. To make matters worse, the ground was hard and cold, like rock. He was glad they had thought to bring gloves with them because they would not have gotten far without them. The cacophony of sound from the prisoners in the two-story hut above them was also a bit disorientating. It took Neumann a moment to adjust to it and get his bearings to head in the proper direction.

It was no problem for Aachen, though. He was a head shorter, so by the time Neumann had crawled a few metres, Aachen had already arrived at the edge of the barracks where the access point was located. The corporal flicked his lighter a couple of times to help orient the sergeant to his location.

Neumann crawled over to the corporal and sat down on the hard ground next to him. "I'm too big for this kind of shit," Neumann said. He spoke quietly, not quite a whisper. He was tempted to speak louder so Aachen could hear him over the echoing of footsteps, conversation, laughter, and snoring above them in the barracks, but Neumann resisted it. Even though it was unlikely that any passing guard would hear them or distinguish their muffled voices from the many others in the hut, he didn't want to take a chance. His years of experience in combat had taught him that even in the loudest battle with artillery firing and landing, one could still hear the smallest sound if it was incongruent enough with the surrounding ambient noise.

"I could continue the mission by myself," Aachen replied in kind. The sergeant could barely hear Aachen and in the darkness, all he could see was the outline of his body and head. Even so, he could hear the corporal's smile in his tone.

"Save the sarcasm and see what's out there, Corporal," Neumann ordered.

Aachen's outline nodded and, very slowly, he pulled on the gap that had been cut into the wood. The panel had been made to look like a natural break and someone in the Escape Committee had installed a hinge on the inside. A one-metre-square section of wood slowly opened inward. It creaked slightly and Aachen stopped. Then, after a breath, he pulled quickly and with a sharp, short creak, the wooden panel swung open.

Although it was after nightfall, the glow from the lights in the camp made the outdoors seem extremely bright when compared to the crawl space. Both Neumann and Aachen instinctively flinched away from the light. After a moment, Aachen slowly stuck his head out to gauge their location.

Just outside the small door, someone had planted a four-metre-long row of raspberry bushes close to the building and the plants had thrived. Although there were no leaves at this time of year, the branches of the plants did give some cover, as did the drifts of snow piled up near the walls.

Aachen turned back to the sergeant. Using hand signals, he indicated that he would leave the crawl space, and when the coast was clear, dash across to the next hut and find its access point. The bushes by the neighbouring hut would provide him with additional cover.

Neumann nodded to offer his approval of the plan. Aachen inched out, crawling on his elbows and knees to stay below the sightline of the bushes. Neumann closed the door slightly behind Aachen to give himself more cover. Still, he could see Aachen.

The corporal crawled along the row of bushes until he reached the end. Light from one of the guard towers circled the area but it didn't reach Aachen's position. This told Neumann someone had spent a lot of time observing the light patterns from the towers and huts and determined the best places to locate these access points. But that didn't surprise him; there was plenty of time for such pursuits in the camp.

As the light moved away, Aachen took a quick look around for any stray scouts. Then, hunched over, he dashed the few metres to the next hut, scuttled behind the bushes there, and crawled along the outside wall. He ran his hands over the wood and looked for a cut that would mark the access point.

Whoever had made the entrance had done a good job concealing it, so it took Aachen a several minutes to find the mark and open the door. He quietly disappeared under the other hut. After a moment, he stuck his head out and waved to the sergeant. Neumann looked around and, seeing no lights or guards, crawled out, quickly closing the panel behind him.

He moved along the ground behind the bushes, taking a quick glance to mark where Aachen was. His ribs hurt as he crawled but he pushed the pain aside. He was determined to complete his mission, as he always had. He remembered the pain of being shot in the arm in the Great War. He had killed a few Brits during an attack and had to make his way through the muck and mayhem of the German trenches to a field hospital while the English peppered his position with mortars and artillery. The ache in his ribs was nothing compared to the burning piece of metal that ripped into his forearm, so he pressed on. If he had been found by the enemy in the trenches, they would have killed him. Here, if he got caught, the worst the Canadians would do was give him a week or so in solitary, which he might actually welcome; it would give him precious time to himself, something he hadn't experienced in a number of years. Save for that time in the summer when the Canadians had tossed him in the cooler for a couple of days. Those days of solace were almost paradise for him.

For a moment, Neumann got lost in his thoughts. The

sound of footfalls in the snow quickly brought him back to the present.

Someone was speaking English with a Canadian accent and moving closer. A second voice replied. Neumann looked over in Aachen's direction. The corporal had a worried look on his face but backed underneath the other hut and shut the hatch. He was safe. Neumann, though, was not.

The sergeant scrambled backwards to see if he could retreat into the crawl space, but the voices were getting closer. There wasn't enough time.

Neumann lay flat on his stomach and covered his head with his arms, almost pushing his nose into the dirt and snow. He lay perfectly still and hoped it was dark enough, and the branches were thick enough, that the Canadians wouldn't notice him lying in the dirt behind a snowdrift. Some of the Veterans Guards had become a bit more lax since they knew the end of the war was close, and they figured the Germans wouldn't consider escaping now. But he couldn't count on that or assume that these guards were among the more complacent ones in the camp.

The Canadians were close enough that Neumann could hear their conversation. One of them mentioned a film he had seen at a local theatre about the bombing of Tokyo. The guard was quite excited by the movie, although he found the romance kind of dull.

Their footsteps crunched in the snow and the voices got louder until the Canadians were parallel with Neumann's position. He pressed his face into the snow and held his breath.

Time seemed to slow down as they walked by him, their voices echoing between the buildings. Neumann had no trouble envisioning the moment of his discovery; rough hands would grab him, an alarm would sound, and their mission would be compromised. Although Aachen wouldn't get caught, once the alarm went off, there would be no way he would make it to the administration building undetected and their investigation into Schlipal's death would be halted yet again.

But the guards' voices passed Neumann and gradually receded into the distance. The sergeant waited a few more seconds before he allowed himself to relax. He took a big, deep breath as quietly as he could before he lifted his arms and looked up. He glanced over to where Aachen was concealed and saw that the corporal had opened the door slightly and was waving him on.

Neumann looked around one last time, then pushed himself up and ran across the no man's land between the huts. He dove to the ground between the wall of the other hut and the bushes, landing on his side, causing a sharp pain to flare from his ribs. He ignored it and scrambled on his knees and elbows to the crawl space entrance. Aachen opened it up completely, grabbed Neumann's arm, and pulled him in. Now safely underneath the hut, they shut the door, blocking out the light.

"That was close," Aachen said, breathing heavily.

Neumann nodded. "You have no idea, Corporal. No idea."

20.

Lying in bed the next morning, Neumann could feel that every muscle and bone in his body ached. They had crawled under and between the camp barracks for more than an hour, but they made it through the rest of their mission without any difficulties after the close call with Canadians. Rier had even caught Neumann's hint at the end of their exchange. Not only had he left the cabinet containing the forms they were looking for unlocked, but he had also kindly retyped them with carbon paper and left one of those carbon copies at the top for Neumann.

The sergeant gave Aachen and Knaup the task of reading and deciphering the forms to see if there was any discrepancy between what was supplied to Schlipal's mess and what was served to the men. And if there was, they would then try to determine who was behind the pilfering.

Unlike the sergeant, Corporal Aachen didn't look any worse for wear after their adventure through the dark. He seemed invigorated by the mission, pleased that he had been able to complete it without slowing down the sergeant. If anything, it was the sergeant who had slowed down the corporal, but Aachen was too polite to say anything about it.

Aachen was not as adept at hiding things from Neumann, especially injuries, but it seemed to the sergeant that the corporal had regained almost 100 percent of his former strength.

"I'll bring you something from breakfast and report to you then if I learn anything new," Aachen had said.

That had been more than two hours ago, but Neumann wasn't concerned about the length of time it was taking. He might be hungry, but he needed some rest. If that didn't help, he would take out Doctor Kleinjeld's box and consider giving himself a little jab to help ease the pain. But the drugs were just a bit too effective for his liking. Best to just lie quiet in his bed with his Karl May novel and his feet sticking out over the edge of the mattress and wait for Aachen and Knaup to return.

A few minutes later, the two corporals were back. Knaup seemed ready to burst with the news of what they had learned and looked at Neumann excitedly. Aachen was barely concealing his own grin and sat on the empty bottom bunk to the right of the sergeant, while Knaup leaned against the end of it.

"From the looks on your faces, you've found what we were looking for," Neumann said, swinging his legs over to sit upright.

They nodded.

"Show me."

Aachen stepped over to sit next to him and Knaup took his place on the opposite bunk.

Aachen pulled the mess inventory records from his pocket. "See here?" he said while pointing at a list of numbers. "Here are the supplies that Schlipal's mess was given in the last four months. It's broken down into each category: flour, sugar, meat, butter, cream, milk—the list goes on. This is what each mess gets every week in deliveries. The numbers for each mess delivery are identical.

"But look here," he flipped to another page. "The total supplies given are relatively consistent with supplies used. There are a few discrepancies, a percentage point or two, probably due to spoilage or minor pilfering, which we expect to see. But that's just August and September, the months after we had our talk with Chef Schlipal. Look at the figures for October and November." Aachen flipped to another page, pointed out another list of numbers. There was a significant decrease from the numbers on the previous pages.

"This is where there's a major difference between the supplies given and the supplies used," Aachen explained. "We did the numbers ourselves and October was at 9.5 percent pilfering while November was at 15 percent."

"Almost to where Schlipal was before we talked to him in June," said Neumann. "And he must have known that somebody would notice, whether he was involved in the process or not."

Aachen nodded. "But with the SS restricting access to the documents, nobody cares about getting caught."

"I don't know why they didn't just fudge the numbers," Knaup said. "That would make more sense to me."

"For once, there's no need to fudge the numbers if nobody with power wishes to do anything about it," Neumann said.

"Also, don't forget, Knaup, these papers show that every time someone uses something in the mess for cooking, they have to record what they used, how much was used, when they used it, and then sign their name," Aachen said, flipping forward to a series of pages that demonstrated this careful documentation. "Every week, these pages are signed off by the head chef before they are submitted. You can do a bit a pilfering, but it's hard to hide it when almost one-fifth of the food is not being used."

Neumann examined these lists, looking at the name on the bottom of ones for the weeks in October and November. He took the papers from Aachen and flipped through the rest, noting the same signature at the bottom of each page.

"What are you seeing, Sergeant?" Aachen asked. Knaup leaned in to try to get a better look.

"For most of the year, all of these sheets were signed by Captain Schlipal, even the ones prior to June when we told him to stop his pilfering or pay the price." He pointed at Schlipal's signature, a big scribble that started with an "S" and could have been anything else afterwards. "But for the last two months, the signature is different. Someone else has been signing off on these numbers."

Neumann pointed at that signature, the handwriting clear and legible. "Looks like we need to have a talk with certain lieutenant."

21.

Neumann, Aachen, and Knaup walked into the chaotic kitchen of Mess #3. Prisoners were preparing for dinner: slicing, dicing, cooking, and frying. Neumann grabbed a worker who was carrying a bowl of sliced onions. "Where can I find Lieutenant Frank?" he asked.

The prisoner gestured over his shoulder towards the mess doors and then went on his way. The three members of Civil Security headed in that direction, Neumann in front, Aachen in the middle, and Knaup bringing up the rear. Despite the chaos of the kitchen, a path cleared for them and they pushed through the doors into the mess.

Lieutenant Frank was sitting at a table near the kitchen doors writing menu items on a piece of paper and smoking. It was the same spot they had found Schlipal's body.

Neumann sat across from the new head chef and gestured

with his eyes for Aachen to sit on the bench next to him. Aachen, in turn, gestured for Knaup to remain standing behind Frank.

The lieutenant glanced up as they took their positions, an amused look on his face. He stopped writing, sat up straight, and took a drag on his cigarette. He blew the smoke in Neumann's direction.

"Okay, you caught me. What did I do?" Frank said jokingly.

Neumann smiled but it didn't reach his eyes. Aachen and Knaup remained passive. "You tell me," Neumann said. "If you confess, then it usually goes easier. Although for some crimes, it's hard to be lenient."

Frank laughed heartily. "You think I killed Schlipal. Why the hell would I do that?"

"You probably had what you considered good reasons," Neumann said. "So please, share them with me."

"I thought it was the other way around. The great detective has to look at all the clues and then confronts the murderer to tell him exactly how and why he killed the victim. Isn't that how it works?"

"I think you may have read too many books. Or seen too many American and British movies at Rhine Hall. They always seem to get it wrong."

"So how does it happen?"

"Oh, there are a few options," Neumann said. "Sometimes I just have to threaten someone and they confess. I find that way much easier."

Frank laughed again, still thinking they were just playing

a game. He looked at Aachen next to him and then Knaup standing behind him. "So this is your threatening gesture? Instructing your corporals to look tough? I've dealt with worse people working in nightclubs in Berlin. Your boys are babies compared to those guys." He finished his cigarette and stubbed it out on the table. He tossed it across the table, purposely missing Neumann but not by much. "I really don't have time for this stupidity. I have a menu to plan for tonight's dinner." Frank moved to get up, but Neumann looked at Knaup. The corporal put his hand on the lieutenant's shoulder and forced him to sit down. "This is preposterous, Neumann. You can't just accuse someone of a crime and push them around."

"Of course I can. The head of Civil Security has many powers."

"Not for long. Things are changing."

"Some people keep telling me that, and if they want to relieve me of my duties I wish they would just get on with it. But until that happens, I'm still the head of Civil Security at this moment in time," Neumann said. "Besides, I never accused you of any crime, you just assumed I did. I find it very interesting that you chose murdering Captain Schlipal as one of them."

"Don't play those games with me," Frank said, rolling his eyes. "I'm not an idiot. Either accuse me of something or let me go."

Neumann shrugged and pulled out the supply information forms. "Very well. These papers are enough to show that you are guilty of pilfering from the German army."

"Where did you get those?"

"That's none of your concern. I have them and they show the facts. Pilfering is a court martial offence."

"If you can find someone to bring charges against me. As I said, Sergeant Neumann, things are changing. No one cares about these matters anymore because those who can do anything about it are thinking about the future. They know the war is coming to an end and they're planning for their lives afterwards. You'd be smart to—"

"Yes, yes," interrupted Neumann. "I've heard the speech many times before from Sergeant Heidfeld. He's always talking about his glorious future and promising the same for us if we work for him. And he's not the only one singing that tune. A lot of people have told me about the glorious future for Germany. When I was young, I believed them wholeheartedly and went to war for them. Then we lost and after years of suffering, more people said Germany had a glorious future. I didn't believe it as much this time but I went to war for them. Again. And we're months away from losing, again. You say there's another glorious future awaiting us after this defeat, but you'll have to excuse me for deciding not to believe these things anymore."

Frank was about to speak, but Neumann waved him off. "I'm tired of talking philosophy with criminals. I just want information."

"You threaten me with this?" Frank said, pointing at the papers. "You're wasting your time. No one cares about pilfering anymore."

"You're right. Everyone's thinking about their futures. But I'm wondering how people are putting things aside for their future. How will they ensure that all the things they are stealing from Germany today and selling to the Canadians on the black market are able to help them when they get back home?"

"We're not stealing from Germany. We're stealing from Canada."

"The Canadians supply the food to feed German prisoners so you are stealing food from the mouths of German soldiers in a time of war."

"No one will bring a charge on me for that."

"Fine," Neumann said. "Then I will pin Schlipal's murder on you."

"You don't have any evidence of that."

"I don't need much. All your staff saw the three of us walk into your kitchen looking for you. They're probably all talking about it while they prepare dinner for the men, speculating about why we came in so earnestly to find you, especially since everyone knows I'm investigating Schlipal's murder. Maybe some of them know you were skimming from the supplies and making a profit. They'll come up with some story about how Schlipal protested about it and you killed him. Or maybe I'll plant that story somewhere and soon the whole camp will know. And you've seen what happens when the camp believes there's been dishonour within our own ranks."

Neumann leaned in. "Do you remember Lieutenant Neuer and what almost happened to him when people believed he killed Captain Mueller? Remember the mob that raced after him, ready to tear him apart, only to be stopped by the Canadians firing their rifles?" Frank's eyes went wide with fear.

"He was lucky he made it to the fence before that mob got to him," Aachen said.

"And he didn't even kill Captain Mueller," Neumann added.

Frank tried to stand up again but Knaup held him down. The lieutenant pushed back but Knaup placed both of his hands on the chef's shoulders to restrain him and Aachen gripped him by his left forearm. Frank stayed where he was.

"See? You're even helping me by struggling against my men. It's showing others in the kitchen that I'm saying something distressing to you and you're trying to get away." Frank looked over and saw that some prisoners in the kitchen were watching the drama unfold. Neumann continued, "They'll draw the obvious conclusion that you killed Schlipal, for whatever reason; because of the pilfering, because you wanted his job, it makes no difference."

Despite the fear in his eyes, Frank remained defiant. "None of them will touch me. I have connections in this camp, powerful connections, as you well know."

"Yes, that Waffen SS lieutenant who tried to stop me from getting these papers. And of course, Sergeant Heidfeld who organizes the black market scheme you're involved with."

Frank nodded. "They won't stand for this. They are not people to tangle with, as you may discover for yourself."

"Probably, but that also goes for you," Neumann said. He reached into his pocket for his cigarette packet. He pulled one out, put it into his mouth, and lit with his lighter. "Word will get back to Heidfeld that we've been questioning you. I could also escort you out of this mess, gently or more firmly, it makes no difference. Maybe talk to some Canadians. Either way, you'll be seen as a liability."

Neumann paused, taking a deep drag on his cigarette. He blew out the smoke. "As I imagine Chef Schlipal was."

The colour drained from Frank's face. His defiant attitude vanished and his eyes pleaded for mercy. "No, please Sergeant. Don't do this to me."

"I'm not doing anything, Lieutenant. I'm just here, talking to you, asking for information. Wondering how you, Heidfeld, and his gang of black marketeers plan to get your proceeds out of the camp so you can live that glorious German future you keep talking about."

Frank slumped down in his seat, shaking his head. "I can't tell you. He'll kill me."

"Probably. But he might kill you even if you don't tell me because he'll believe you did. So you pretty much have no choice in the matter." Neumann took another drag on his cigarette and nodded to Knaup and Aachen to release the chef. They did but Frank made no move to get away. He was a defeated man, and out of options.

"If you help me," Neumann continued, "and tell me what I need to know, I can promise you two things."

Frank looked up, hope glimmering in his eyes.

"First, I will get Corporals Knaup and Aachen to escort you to the Canadians and they will ask to put you in protective custody. You'll be safe there until the end of the war. Who knows? Maybe the Canadians will let you stay so you can avoid any prosecution you might face back in Germany."

"Lieutenant Neuer is there, and though he finds it boring, he's pleased to be alive," added Aachen.

"What's the other promise?" Frank asked.

"I will do what I can to disrupt Heidfeld's operation and his hold on this camp."

"That won't be easy. You have no idea who's with him and who's not." And his reach is broader than you know. He has commandeered a whole classroom to store many of the goods he's mustered.

Neumann made a mental note about the classroom. "That's true, but I've survived two world wars, so far. A bunch of criminals don't scare me." Neumann leaned forward and placed his hand over Frank's. It was a gentle touch, meant to calm the chef, not scare him. Like many chefs' hands, Frank's was marked with various cuts and scars from working in a kitchen with sharp knives and hot objects.

"Tell me, Lieutenant Frank, how do the proceeds leave the camp?"

Frank sighed. "There's a concert for the civilians in the city, in Lethbridge," he whispered. "For Christmas. One of the musicians will smuggle some of our money out, as well as some other 'very lucrative goods,' as Heidfeld put it."

"And what are these 'lucrative goods'?" Neumann asked.

"I don't know. He didn't tell me. But he says we should make a lot of money from it."

"And what will they do with this money?"

"He has a Canadian with contacts in Switzerland or Austria who can deposit the money in a numbered account."

Neumann nodded, surprised. It was a rather simple yet ingenious plan. "Do you have a name for this musician?" Neumann asked. "Or the Canadian?"

Frank shook his head. "No, we were never told any names, just how it would be done."

"And Heidfeld trusts this Canadian?"

"Trust? No. But he has something on him, probably. I don't know."

"Sounds like Heidfeld," Aachen said. "If you won't help him when he asks, he resorts to threats and blackmail."

Neumann nodded. "Thank you, Lieutenant Frank. I appreciate the information. Corporals Aachen and Knaup will now escort you to the Canadians. I'm afraid there's no time to gather any of your gear from your bunk. If you want, I can drop it off later."

Frank didn't reply. He just stood up and allowed himself to be steered towards the mess exit by the two corporals.

When they were halfway across the room, Neumann called out, "Lieutenant Frank. One more thing?"

The three men stopped. Frank turned slowly to face the sergeant.

"Did you steal the dagger from Sergeant Hill, or did he give it to you? Or was it stolen by someone else before you got your hands on it?"

The lieutenant's eyes went wide in surprise as he collapsed to the floor.

22.

Knaup reacted quickly and hauled Frank back to his feet.

"How did you know?" the lieutenant stammered. His knees had given out beneath him and he struggled now to regain his balance.

Aachen didn't move to help, but he gave the sergeant a questioning look.

Neumann nodded. "I'll tell you later," he said.

Suddenly, the lieutenant was down again, this time bringing Knaup to the ground with him where the two of them struggled. Knaup may have been younger and stronger, but the chef was more desperate, kicking and swinging wildly with his fists. Knaup raised his hands to defend himself but Frank used that moment to throw the corporal back against a bench. Aachen bent down to try to restrain the chef, but Frank's foot caught the corporal in the face, knocking him to the ground.

With both corporals on the floor, Frank scrambled to his feet and rushed to the mess exit, knocking over a few benches in the process. As he pushed through the doors, he collided with a group of prisoners but fought his way past them and was gone. Angry voices shouted after him outside.

Knaup jumped to his feet to chase after him, but Neumann, who had not moved from his spot once the melee started, shouted at him to stop.

"But he's getting away, Sergeant," Knaup protested excitedly. "I can catch him."

Neumann shook his head. "Don't bother. He's in a prisoner-of-war camp; where can he go? Help Aachen instead."

Knaup glanced back at the mess doors, thinking for a moment about disregarding the sergeant's orders, but he changed his mind. He went over to Aachen who was sitting up, holding his face. Blood was streaming from his nose.

Neumann pulled out a handkerchief and handed it to Aachen to stem the flow of blood.

"Next time, I would appreciate some notice when you're going to accuse someone of murder," he said as he pressed the cloth to his face and pinched the bridge of his nose.

"It came to me suddenly. I noticed something about Frank when we were first here with Schlipal's body and I saw it again today. I only made the connection as you were leading him away."

"I was here both times and didn't notice anything," Knaup said. "What was it?"

"His hands," replied Neumann, holding up his hand and

pointing to the area below his second row of knuckles. "When we first talked with Frank after seeing Schlipal's body, I saw red marks on his hand. I thought it was from his work, from burning himself when he got me that hot towel from the oven. But then today, those same marks are now bruises which probably came from repeatedly stabbing the push dagger into Schlipal's chest and back. He probably tried to take it out but, as Corporal Knaup can attest, it took a lot of work for me to remove it. Lieutenant Frank probably panicked when the knife wouldn't budge and left it there."

"And who's Sergeant Hill?"

"A Canadian soldier that I met at the hospital. He had a holster that looked like it held such a dagger but it was empty," Neumann said. "So he probably gave Frank the knife, which would make him the Canadian contact he was talking about. Or someone stole the dagger from the guard."

"Who?" Knaup asked.

But Neumann waved the question away. "I think we all know who. But come on Knaup. I need you to get Aachen to the hut so he can clean himself up."

Neumann helped Aachen stand up. He tried to do a quick examination of the corporal's face to see if his injury was serious.

"I'm fine," Aachen said, pushing the sergeant away. "I've been hit harder in wrestling practice. I just need to clean up." Aachen slowly weaved his way through the mess towards the kitchen. Neumann gestured for Knaup to follow him.

"Are you going after Lieutenant Frank?" Knaup asked. "You should wait until we're done. I can help you."

"There's no need to go after Frank. I'm sure someone will take care of him." Neumann turned on his heel and headed towards the mess doors. "I've got to find Liszt so I can join his orchestra."

23.

Neumann stood at the back of Rhine Hall, listening to the orchestra rehearse. They played a medley of compositions suitable for Christmas, ending with Tchaikovsky's "Waltz of the Flowers." Neumann felt that the finale for Beethoven's Symphony No. 5, which they played prior to *The Nutcracker Suite,* would have been more suitable coming from an orchestra made up of captured German soldiers—especially since Tchaikovsky was a Russian composer. But then again, "Waltz of the Flowers" was a more pleasing melody.

The Canadians would like it; the more astute ones would also notice the order. Camp Command might notice it as well, but there was little they could do now to stop it. Even they knew the war was coming to an end and clamping down on something as non-important as music wouldn't make sense.

All around the hall, which was probably the largest building of its kind in western Canada, capable of seating five thousand people, scores of prisoners were busy cleaning, polishing, practicing, and decorating for the annual Christmas concert. The work they had done was impressive, enough to equal some of the decorations he had seen in Frankfurt prior to the war when he was still talking to and visiting his sister at Christmas.

The quality of their work didn't surprise him though; the prisoners had plenty of time on their hands and of the 12,000 soldiers in the camp, many had professional backgrounds in theatre, architecture, and design and were willing to plan and create the decorations needed for a hall this size.

When the orchestra finished the medley and Liszt had given them leave to take a break, Neumann approached the front of the hall to talk to the conductor. When the other soldiers in his path saw him striding purposefully in Liszt's direction, they moved out of his way, or waited for him to pass.

"Conductor Liszt," Neumann called out as he came within a few metres of the stage.

Liszt was gathering his score but turned to the sound of Neumann's voice. He smiled when he recognized the sergeant. "Ahh, Neumann. Have you decided to take me up on my offer to play this Christmas? I'll admit it's a bit late, but we could make room for you. I'd have to put you as a fourth chair because of that, but with practice you could work your way up to third, or even second."

Neumann smiled, and stopped next to Liszt. "That is what I came to talk to you about. Joining the orchestra."

Liszt beamed at the sergeant, but his delight was quickly replaced with suspicion. "What are you on about, Neumann? I'm not in the mood for joking."

"I'm not joking, Liszt. I wish to join your orchestra. In fact," he paused and leaned in, "I'm insisting on it."

Liszt swore at Neumann, grabbed the rest of his pages, hugging them to his chest, and turned to walk away. Neumann grabbed the conductor by the arm and turned Liszt to face him again. The papers fell out of Liszt's arms and onto the floor. "I'm afraid I'm not asking, Conductor."

Liszt let out a bitter laugh as he bent to pick up his music. He gathered the pages, again hugging them in his arms, and stood up. "If you wished to join my orchestra because of the music, I would let you in. I would welcome you and make you a third instead of a fourth, even though you haven't played in years. But I believe you have other reasons to join and I won't have it. I won't."

"You have no choice in the matter," Neumann said. "I need to find out who killed Captain Schlipal."

"How can joining the orchestra help with that? Do you suspect one of my musicians?" Liszt asked with a dry laugh. "If so, then you've gone crazy. My boys are harmless. They play their music and stay out of the stupidity in the camp. They want no part of it."

Neumann leaned in close to the conductor and placed a hand on his shoulder. "You have a performance outside the camp tomorrow night," he whispered. "I need to join you for that performance."

Liszt froze in surprise, then stepped back, horrified. "You

wish to leave this camp to find Schlipal's killer?" the conductor hissed. "That's insane."

"It's necessary."

"No, it's insane! You're a German prisoner of war—you can't just find a way to leave the camp to investigate a murder. The Canadians will catch you if you try. They might even kill you."

"That's a chance I'll have to take."

"I won't allow it," Liszt said, shaking his head.

"As I said, I'm not asking, I'm ordering you to do so."

"You're a sergeant and I'm a captain; maybe you've forgotten that."

"I'm the head of Civil Security for this camp; maybe you've forgotten *that*."

Liszt shook off Neumann's hand. Neumann stepped right up to Liszt, towering over the conductor. "I'll make sure your orchestra never leaves this camp until the war is over," Neumann said.

Liszt's eyes went wide. After a moment, he said, "If it stops you from doing something stupid, all the better. I don't care."

Neumann chuckled, but it wasn't a pleasant one. "Of course you care. I know you, Liszt, and I know this is one of the most important concerts of your career. Sure it's not Berlin, but it's your only chance to show the Canadians how good you truly are. How good we all are. That we aren't just the enemy, aren't just a bunch of captured, defeated German soldiers. I know you want to show them that a bunch of POWs are part of the best orchestra they have ever seen. The best orchestra they will probably ever see in their lives."

Liszt said nothing yet the look on his face told Neumann that he had hit a chord. "So, if you don't let me in for this performance, you'll never get the chance to do that. And any pride you have in your boys and their abilities will mean nothing because no one outside the camp will see their talents."

Liszt shook his head, blinking back tears. "And you're willing to do this to me, your friend, for Schlipal? He's worth more to you than our friendship? More than your life?"

Neumann nodded.

"But he was an asshole and a black marketeer. He took advantage of us for his own profit and he paid the price. You don't need to add your name to the bill."

"I know what he was. I know he profited from us in the camp, but on the battlefield, he made sure we were fed, that our rations were up to snuff, that we had enough to eat when we went out to fight. He was a total asshole sometimes, but he was a German asshole," Neumann said. "This has nothing to do with the man, who he was, or what he did. It's about a German solider being murdered by one of his own country-men, one who was working with the enemy."

Neumann grabbed Liszt by the shoulders. He leaned his face in close. "And that I cannot stand," he whispered harshly. "That, I cannot allow. We cannot allow."

Liszt blinked. "But why involve me and my orchestra? We just want to play music."

Neumann gently released Liszt. "Not all of you," he said.

"What are you talking about?" Liszt leaned in, whispering. "Are you accusing one of my boys of being involved in this?"

"Maybe not in the murder itself, but yes. Someone in your orchestra is close to what killed Schlipal."

Liszt's face went red with anger. "Who?" he hissed. "Tell me which one and I'll tan his hide. I'll break his arms and fingers so he'll never play music again. Tell me."

Neumann recoiled from Liszt's outburst. "I don't know who," he said quietly. "And if I did, I wouldn't tell you because I need them to stay in your orchestra so they can leave the camp. That's where they are meeting the Canadian, or Canadians, that are helping them."

"And you wish to join us in order to find them? And stop them?"

Neumann nodded.

"And then you'll let me know so I can deal with them later?"

Neumann nodded. "Although they might be in protective custody."

Liszt frowned. "If you don't allow me the chance to get revenge, then I won't let you into the orchestra."

"Like I said, you have no choice in the matter. I'm joining," Neumann said. Then he smiled. "Besides, there is a good chance that whoever in your orchestra is involved with this won't appreciate me interrupting their plans. So they might try to stop me. And that will go badly for them."

Liszt nodded. "I'll get you a viola." He poked Neumann in the chest with his finger. "But you must practice. Even if there are only two days and you'll be a fourth, I'm going to expect you to be ready. You understand?"

Neumann nodded. "I'll be ready."

24.

Neumann sat on the edge of his bunk with a viola case resting on his lap. The case was dusty and old; the leather was cracked and peeling, one of the clasps was missing, and the handle, while still attached, was broken. Neumann ran a hand along the case, clearing the dust off. He paused, took a deep breath, and opened it up.

The viola was nothing special; some mass-produced instrument with a faded finish and made of cheap wood that was splintered in several places. It was made in the classic Mittenwald style so it might have been fabricated in Europe, but he doubted it. There were, however, four good strings on it, probably replaced by whoever donated it to the camp. Neumann gently plucked the D string, but it was so out of tune that the note it gave was almost unrecognizable.

After a moment, Neumann lifted the viola out of the case

with two hands underneath, cradling it like a priest presenting a baby to God after its baptism. He set the viola down beside him and pulled out the bow.

Like the viola, the wood of the bow was cheap with a faded finish. But the bow hair was relatively new, also probably just changed before being donated. He set the bow down on the bunk, to his right this time, then closed the case and set it on the floor. He picked up the viola and placed it on his lap, looking at it, as if he was unsure what to do next.

"It's been a long time," he said out loud to no one in particular.

"I think you're making a mistake," Aachen said. The corporal was leaning against the wall of the hut, his glance alternating between looking out the window next to him to looking at the sergeant. His nose was red and swollen. He was clearly not pleased with the sergeant's plan. "Remember the last time you decided to face someone alone? You came out of it with several broken ribs and a broken arm. You were lucky to have survived."

"That's because I wasn't completely sure he was the murderer and I did not expect him to attack when confronted," said Neumann. "This time, I will be prepared." He plucked the C string. It was closer in tune, but not by much. "And I'm not looking to take anyone in because that would be impossible. All I'm looking forward to is disrupting the meeting."

"They probably know you'll make an attempt to do so," Aachen said. "The first place Frank probably ran to was Heidfeld's hut to tell him you now know everything."

"You're probably right, Corporal. I'm glad you're getting back to your old self again."

"Then listen to me when I say this is a mistake," Aachen said with a frown. "You should not do this. We already know that he killed Schlipal. And even though Frank's probably in hiding, or soon to be dead since Heidfeld isn't a fan of mistakes that cost him, or the people that make them, we have our answer."

"Yes, we know it was Frank who killed Schlipal, but he was only the instrument, much like this viola. We don't know who put him up to it."

"It was Heidfeld."

"Yes, of course it was Heidfeld. But who is the German musician helping Heidfeld? And who is he meeting outside the camp after the concert? Who is the Canadian? Why do they trust him?"

Aachen looked out the window. Light snow flurries whirled around outside. A group of prisoners with shovels and brooms were working to keep the pathways between the barracks clear. Yet each time they removed the snow from one path, it was soon covered again by the falling snow and they had to go back and clear it once more. They didn't seem to mind because at least it gave them something to do. Aachen felt the urge to go help them, to be a normal, dull prisoner and forget all this business with criminals.

"That's why this is a mistake." Aachen said. "Going outside the camp to confront a Canadian, even a criminal Canadian, is more dangerous than confronting someone inside the camp, even someone like Heidfeld. At least in the camp you have people like me and Knaup to help you. And whoever else you've enlisted to help us because of the size of Heidfeld's group."

Neumann looked up in surprise. "What makes you think I've enlisted others to help us deal with Heidfeld?"

"Heidfeld has a lot of power in this camp, and he has a lot of people working for or with him. Like that Waffen SS lieutenant. And we're only three, with Knaup being the only one who is at full strength." Aachen shrugged and gave a heavy sigh. His breath froze on the window and he used the warm palm of his hand to melt it so he could continue to watch the regular prisoners work outside. "So getting help from, let's just say, a legion of other soldiers, makes a lot sense."

Neumann stared at Aachen for several seconds. He tried to will the corporal to look at him, but Aachen seemed content to watch the soldiers outside the window. Neumann then turned his gaze to Corporal Knaup, who was sitting on the top bunk next to Aachen. "This is why one should never underestimate someone like Corporal Aachen," Neumann told him. "Here you are, thinking you're doing something in secret, but he's already got it all figured out."

Aachen turned away from the window and took the two steps to stand at the end of Neumann's bunk. "So this is why you should listen to me when I say your plan is a mistake," Aachen said, gesturing at the viola sitting on Neumann's lap. "This concert idea of yours can only end badly. You'll either get captured by the Canadians and thrown in the cooler, or someone will try to kill you. But unlike last time, you'll be outside the camp and there will be no one to help you."

"I'm prepared for that. You don't have to worry about me, Corporal."

"Of course I do, Sergeant. It's my job as your second-in-command of this squad to worry about you. That's why I followed you the other day to see where were going but left when I realized you were heading into the legionnaire hut. It was a smart idea to solicit their help in case we have to face Heidfeld head on. But it's also my job to question you if I believe you're recklessly heading into battle without backup from your squad."

"I've thought it through carefully, Corporal. You've served with me a long enough to know I'm never reckless, especially during an incursion into enemy territory."

"But those were never solo missions into enemy territory," Aachen said, pointing at himself and Knaup. "If something happens, we can't help you."

"I know that, Aachen," Neumann said with a sigh. "But there's no other option. I can't bring you and Knaup along because you can't play well enough to fit into the orchestra."

"The other option would be not to go. To stay in the camp." Aachen backed away and returned to the wall to look out the window.

"That's not an option. That's surrendering. I can't do that."

"We surrendered once. We can do it again."

"We only did that because continuing to fight was futile. Unlike our Japanese allies, we don't fight to the last man or rush into suicide attacks. We all would have died useless and dishonourable deaths if we kept fighting in Africa."

Aachen said nothing. He shook his head and looked out the window.

"Listen Klaus. I hear what you're saying. I know we've discovered who killed Schlipal but this is bigger than that. We can't let Heidfeld continue his operation; killing people indiscriminately, ordering hits, and working with Canadians outside the camp with impunity. He came to you last summer, asked you to lose in your match to Neuer and you refused. He even tried to kill you in the shower but you fought back against him. And even after they beat you, you still tried to win your match, despite your injuries. You know why you did that, Aachen? Because I do. And so does everyone in the camp, right Knaup?"

Knaup nodded. "Corporal Aachen is an honourable man, that's why."

"Exactly," Neumann said, pointing at Knaup. "You're a strong fighter, a great warrior in battle, Klaus, but you're an honourable man. And honourable men like you must stand against dishonourable men like Heidfeld. If we let Heidfeld win this one, he will not stop. He will continue to believe he has the power in the camp, and he will abuse it until the end of the war. And after. So while we will probably lose this war, we must do our best to come out of it with some honour. That won't happen if we let Heidfeld get his way. Which is why I have to go out of the camp and break up this deal he's planned, no matter the cost."

Aachen was silent for a few moments. He sighed and paused before he spoke. "I may not agree with you, Sergeant, but I do know when you make up your mind about an approach for battle, you cannot be dissuaded. Even though we may disagree, once you have a plan in place I have to trust you to implement it. And so far that trust has paid off." Aachen turned his gaze from the window to Neumann. "I guess I'm just feeling disappointed that I can't help you in this battle, just as I can't help the German armies back home who are fighting the Allies."

"That's understandable, Aachen. We all feel this way. But you know me. I've faced many battles even worse than this alone, against enemy soldiers, and so far I've survived."

Aachen sighed. "I know, Sergeant. But just be careful."

Neumann nodded. "I can't promise you that, but I will protect myself, you can be sure." He looked down at the viola on his lap. "It's this thing I'm worried about. I'm supposed to fit into Liszt's orchestra but I haven't played in years."

"I didn't know you even played, Sergeant," Knaup said.

"You probably thought I was a tough, uncultured asshole with no redeeming qualities, right Knaup?" Neumann said with a smile.

Knaup stammered, flushing red.

Neumann laughed.

"Don't worry, Dieter," Aachen said, "everyone thinks that about Sergeant Neumann. I served with him in North Africa for a long time and even I didn't know he played an instrument."

"I'm not even sure I still can," Neumann said, holding the

viola vertically. "I can't even remember the last time I played one. In 1938, or maybe '37. I don't know. I've been fighting for so long that it feels like more than ten lifetimes ago."

"Maybe it's like a bike, Sergeant," Knaup said. "Maybe all you have to do is start and it will come back."

Neumann shrugged, turning the instrument over in his hands to look at it from different angles. "Well, for starters, let's just see if I remember how to tune the damn thing."

25.

Veterans Guards loaded the musicians up into the back of a truck, a three-tonner Neumann figured, similar to the Opel Blitz but more square at the front. Still, it was just another variation of the standard two- to three-tonne trucks used by the military to move men and supplies all over the world in this war, no matter what side they were fighting on.

The other musicians were a bit surprised to see Sergeant Neumann standing in line with them to load up, but they said nothing. It was common knowledge amongst the musicians that Conductor Liszt had been courting Neumann for months to play in the orchestra. They probably figured Liszt had finally convinced him.

Neumann didn't care what the other musicians thought. He was not there to impress them. He would play the best he could, even if his practices over the past few days showed that his abilities weren't as good as they were years ago.

When it was Neumann's turn, Sergeant Murray froze, clipboard in hand.

"Fuck me," Murray said. "What the hell is he doing here?"

"Sergeant Neumann is my fourth viola. Not the best player in the camp but suitable for our needs." Liszt tried to act nonchalant about Neumann's presence, but he wasn't entirely convincing.

"He's not on my list," Murray said, looking at his roster.

"He's a last minute addition. I've been demanding that he join my orchestra for months and he finally agreed."

"Bullshit. Something stinks about this." Murray pushed Liszt aside and stepped towards Neumann, poking him on the shoulder. Murray was probably one of the few men in the camp, Canadian or German, who was almost as big as Neumann. "What's your game, Neumann?"

"As conductor Liszt said, I am the fourth viola for the group. I just joined last week."

"Bullshit."

"No bullshit. I've been playing the viola since I was a lad. Even won some competitions. However, certain things got in the way of pursuing it as a professional career."

"Like what?"

"Like the war you and I fought in against each other. It was very inconvenient for my music career," he said. "Much like this one."

"Well, we didn't start that one, we just finished it," Murray sneered. "Much like this one."

"True. And seeing that the end of this war is near, I became convinced that I should revisit my old hobby so I can take it up again when I get back home. Music always gave me solace so I decided to accept Conductor Liszt's offer to play in his orchestra."

"Fuck me. You sure are full of bullshit."

"You're probably correct, Sergeant Murray. My skills have diminished, but if the conductor believes I can play, then who am I to argue?"

Murray moved closer so his face was only inches from Neumann's. The sergeant did not budge or break eye contact with the big Canadian guard. "You can't play. This is just some kind of scheme you've got cooking."

The conductor moved towards the two men. "Sergeant Neumann is a decent amateur—"

"Shut the fuck up, Liszt. I'm not talking to you." The conductor backed away. Murray stared at Neumann for several more seconds, looking for some sign of deception, but Neumann showed him nothing. After a moment, the Canadian took a step back. "Okay, if you say you can play, then play. Open up that case and play something."

"Here, Sergeant Murray? That's most inopportune, we have a schedule to keep," said Liszt, trying to put a bit of officer command in his voice.

Murray ignored him. "Play or I'll send you to the cooler for two weeks. Maybe more."

Neumann paused, then shrugged. He took a step back and set his case on the open bed of the truck. He clicked the one working latch and opened the case. In the guard tower to the right, he heard the sound of someone cocking a rifle. Neumann did his best not to react to it.

He pulled the bow out, tightened it, and then took out the viola, tucking it between his shoulder and chin. He looked at Sergeant Murray. "Any requests?" he asked.

"Just play the fucking thing," the Canadian growled at him.

Neumann hitched his arm slightly and started to play. At first he just ran up and down several scales, moved onto some warm up flourishes, and then played several bars of Tchaikovsky's "Waltz of the Flowers," which was the final suite of the night's performance. He played the first viola part, not his own, because he had to ensure that the Canadian sergeant heard a melody, whether he recognized it or not.

Neumann did take pleasure in seeing the surprise on the big Canadian's face. Murray stepped back. A couple of the guards in the tower applauded. Neumann bowed slightly and moved to put his instrument away, loosening the bow before closing the case. He had made a number of mistakes in the piece but they didn't need to know that.

"Okay, you can fucking play," Murray said, back to his normal, obnoxious self. "But if I get wind of any monkey business from you, I'll shoot you myself." He stepped away from Neumann and pointed towards the truck and the other prisoners. "The same goes for all you fucking Krauts. We'll be outside the camp so all the guards will be armed. And we'll have a jeep in front of you and one behind. So if you fuckers make any move to escape, you'll be shot. You understand me?"

The Germans who could understand English nodded. The others looked to their counterparts for translation, but even those prisoners understood the meaning of Murray's tone, even if they didn't understand the words.

Neumann climbed aboard the truck and took a seat on a bench to the right. Even though it was a tight squeeze, the other musicians deliberately kept their distance from him. Like the Canadians, most of them were not pleased by the sergeant's last minute addition to their group.

Neumann ignored them, shutting his eyes, and thought about the concert, wondering which musician, or even musicians, were in on Heidfeld's plan.

With the truck finally loaded, Conductor Liszt climbed in, taking a seat at the end of the bench on the left side. The guards closed the gate and secured the canopy flap so the Germans couldn't see outside.

Then the truck jerked forward, slowly moving through the first inside gate. After a couple of seconds, it stopped. Neumann heard the gate bang closed behind them. A moment later, a Canadian, one Neumann didn't recognize, flipped up the canvas flap and looked in. He pointed a flashlight into the back, moving his light over every single prisoner in the truck, counting them out loud. Those with instruments small enough to hold on their laps or in their hands did so. Bigger ones, like cases for bass drums, some larger brass instruments, and even a bassoon, sat on the floor of the truck. The guard inspected them with his light. When he was satisfied, the Canadian left, closing the canopy behind him.

"Okay, ready to go," he shouted. There was a bang on the side of the truck as he slapped his hand against it. "Move it out."

Again, the sound of a gate opening—the main entrance gate—and the truck jerked forward. It started slow at first and then picked up speed as it carried Neumann and the other prisoners into the town the Canadians called Lethbridge. No one spoke a single word during the entire trip.

Neumann had been outside the camp previously. Even though Captain Mueller had been murdered, his death was still considered an honourable one. When he was buried in the cemetery next to the camp, the funeral had full military honours, even led by a Canadian pipe band. Neumann had served as part of the honour guard and as a pallbearer. He had marched out of the camp for the funeral.

There had been a second funeral that summer, but there was no honour guard for the dead man. The official story was that he killed himself because he had supported those who had tried and failed to assassinate the Führer. Neumann had been in hospital at that time, beaten almost to death by the man buried at that second funeral.

For most of the prisoners jammed into that truck, it was their first time outside the camp since they had arrived. And though it was obvious by the way they looked at the canopy at the back of the truck, no one dared to peek out for fear of getting a bullet between their eyes.

26.

The concert, held in a large indoor sports arena that smelled of sweat and livestock, went reasonably well. It seemed that the entire town had come to the event because every seat in the building was occupied. The Canadians booed the camp orchestra when they were introduced, and there was some jeering during the first few minutes of the performance. But the musicians showed great composure and discipline. The jeers soon faded and as the orchestra finished the final notes of the concert, the crowd applauded heartily, clearly impressed by the musicians' abilities.

Liszt bowed deeply, trying to look dignified, but he could barely hold back his smile.

Neumann knew his own performance had had many mistakes, but he was not the only one. In each piece, musicians missed or screeched notes and lost their timing for a second.

For the most part, however, these small errors were not noticed by the crowd. Liszt had smartly featured several of the more talented musicians—actual professionals—as soloists and kept the overall orchestra performance to relatively easy and known melodies.

The concert was a success and in their dressing room, a place normally reserved for athletes, the musicians were ebullient. A few from the brass section and one of the percussionists had smuggled some of the homemade prison brew in their cases and these bottles were passed around.

They even included Neumann in their celebration, handing him a bottle as it made its way around. Neumann took a small sip; he did not want to overconsume. Lieutenant Gottfried Pfiefel, the first viola and the most accomplished musician in the orchestra—before going to war he was the first viola and assistant musical director of the Symphony in Hamburg—came over to sit by Neumann.

Pfiefel was about thirty years old, of average height, but a little thick around the waist, not unlike many of the other prisoners after more than a year in the camp. He had commanded a mortar platoon and had lost his left eye during the latter part of the African Campaign so he wore a black eyepatch.

"That was a remarkable solo," Neumann said as Pfiefel sat down. "It's been a long time since I've seen such work by a violist. Thank you for accepting me into your group."

Pfiefel accepted the compliment and thanks with some feigned deference. "I had no say in accepting you into my section, Sergeant Neumann. You were forced on me by Conductor

Liszt. However, I must admit, I was surprised by your ability. You were …" Pfiefel searched for a word, "… tolerable. I would not mind if you continued to play with us in the future."

Neumann accepted the compliment with grace. He knew he wasn't even close to Pfiefel's ability and talent, even when he had been considered a "talented youngster," so he knew the violist meant well by the comment. They chatted a bit longer, but it was obvious that Pfiefel did not wish to linger.

Neumann didn't mind. He was watching to see if any of the musicians would attempt to leave the room to liaise with a Canadian. There was an armed guard outside the door of the dressing room, and from the time the POWs were loaded into the truck in the camp, there had been no chance for anyone to have left the group to make contact.

Neumann did not expect the meeting to occur before the concert because there was no time and too much concern from the Canadians about the concert being held outside the camp. Now that the show was over and drinks were being passed around, things were more relaxed. There was a chance that the Canadians might let down their guard sometime between now and the trip back to the camp. There was also the possibility that whoever the contact was from the Canadian side would create a situation so that one of the Germans had to be drawn away from the group. Even if it was only a small window of time, it would probably be enough to make the connection.

Neumann intended to stop this from happening, so that no goods would be passed from the camp to the outside.

But nothing happened in the sports arena. The prisoners

were given another ten minutes to celebrate their performance and then Sergeant Murray entered the room.

"Okay, you fucking Krauts," he shouted. Time to go home." Murray was not armed as he stood in the doorway but there were three Canadian guards standing behind him who were.

A couple of the prisoners shouted insults at Murray in German but they didn't faze the Canadian at all. He called them something worse in German, showing that he had picked up select words from his charges.

The prisoners laughed at the insult, pleased that they had had some influence on the big Canadian guard. They started to gather their instruments and coats and filed out of the room towards the waiting trucks. Neumann joined the group, his senses hyperalert. This would be the time, he thought. Something might happen. He expected that someone would be singled out, maybe even more than one person to conceal the identity of the actual German contact.

But nothing happened. The Veterans Guards shouted at the prisoners to hurry, as they always did. A group of Canadian civilians stood outside the arena in the fading daylight watching the spectacle of German POWs being marched towards the truck. A few adolescent Canadian boys shouted insults at the prisoners and some of the prisoners jeered back. Neumann was certain this was the moment some prisoners would be taken out of line for "punishment." Yet there was nothing. Sergeant Murray shouted at both groups to "shut the fuck up." The commanding boom of his voice did the trick.

The prisoners and their equipment were all loaded into the

truck without difficulty. Everyone was noted and accounted for by Liszt and Murray. The convoy then headed back to the camp.

After driving a short distance, their truck slowed to a stop. The musicians dared not look out the covered windows to see what had brought the truck to a halt. They could hear some conversation, a bit of an argument, it seemed, but not heated. Neumann tensed, ready to react in case someone was removed from the truck.

But the discussion ceased and the truck jerked forward again, resuming its journey to the camp. Suddenly, the driver made a sharp turn that Neumann didn't remember during the trip into town and the truck stopped once again, idling for several moments.

Outside, he heard someone barking orders but could not make out the actual words. The flap of the truck opened up at the same time the gate was unlatched.

"It's your lucky day, boys," said one of the guards Neumann didn't recognize. "Someone from the Chamber of Commerce told the camp commander he was impressed with your show and convinced him to give you guys a reward. So step on out all nice like."

The prisoners who understood were pleased yet also confused. Others who didn't understand were worried. But they understood what was expected of them as soon as the first musician stepped out from the truck.

"It's a movie theatre," he shouted. "We are going to see a movie."

"Better not be Canadian propaganda," said one of the men. "I'm sick and tired of those things. I want to see John Wayne."

The Germans were filed out of the truck and then into theatre quickly to limit their exposure to the town. Not that it mattered; from the few seconds Neumann was outside, he could see that the street was deserted. But he didn't look around much, or even glance at the marquee to see what was playing. He kept his eyes fixed on everyone who went in. The exchange would happen here. Somewhere in the theatre, sometime during the showing of the movie. He just had to be on the lookout for it.

27.

The Germans sat in two rows in the middle of the empty theatre. Guards stood at all the exits and at the ends of the two rows to prevent anyone from leaving their seat. Neumann made sure he got a seat on the end in case something happened. Once they settled in, Sergeant Murray walked into a row in front of them and stopped in the middle. He turned to the prisoners, his rifle resting on his crossed arms.

"Against my better judgment, our camp commander was persuaded by a bunch of the town mucky-mucks to reward you Krauts for the concert," he said. "I told them it was a mistake and I still think it is, but I'm only a fucking sergeant and was overruled by an officer who should know better but doesn't."

The Germans who understood English laughed at that. Neumann couldn't help but smile. No matter what side one fought on in a war, the disdain many enlisted men felt for officers was universal. Even the officers in the orchestra knew this and laughed.

"We're going to let you watch a bit of a movie. Not sure how much but don't get too comfortable. This not your home and you are not welcome here. If any one of you tries to run, I will shoot you."

One of the percussionists who had smuggled in the alcohol and had consumed too much stood up and saluted. "Heil Hitler!" he said. Some laughed, more Canadians than Germans. Murray smiled and pointed his rifle at the prisoner. The soldier's friends quickly pulled him back into his seat. Someone in the row behind him gave him a slap across the back of the head.

Satisfied his orders had been heard and understood, Murray moved out of the way. The room went dark and the movie started.

It wasn't the first movie Neumann had seen while he was a prisoner. The Canadians were always showing them movies in Rhine Hall, mostly propaganda films that vilified the Germans and the Führer and exalted the Allies. This was not surprising. Most of the prisoners didn't really watch those movies even though they were forced to sit in the hall. Every few weeks, the Canadians would bring in a real movie, one with real actors and a real story, usually something American; a romance, a detective story, sometimes a war movie. No one minded because any movie, save for the propagandist ones, was a break from the monotony of the camp.

This was the first time in almost a decade that Neumann,

and probably every other German in the orchestra, had seen an actual movie in an actual theatre. The seats were soft cloth, probably the softest thing Neumann had sat on in a decade, too.

The movie was about an air raid the Americans had done over Tokyo. The beginning of the picture was a bit dull, about airmen learning how to fly with a story of romance between one of the pilots and his newly pregnant wife. Neumann expected that this pilot would die or get injured as a dramatic ploy to make the audience cry.

The musicians were a more cultured lot than the average prisoner, but even they jeered and booed at the movie's early scenes. The Veterans Guards shouted at them to be quiet and the prisoners obeyed. A few minutes later, they would start again, laughing and making rude comments when the pilot slept in a separate bed than his wife.

"How did he get her pregnant?" someone shouted in German. It was the drunk percussionist. "Fuck her from across the room?" The other men roared with laughter.

"Maybe he's got a big American prick," shouted the prisoner sitting next to him, also a percussionist.

"Americans don't have big pricks!" retorted his drunk neighbour.

"How do you know? Have you seen a lot of American pricks?" More laughter.

"Only the ones I've shot off."

"With your rifle or your hand?" A big bout of laughter followed that one. Even Neumann and the prisoner who was the butt of the joke couldn't help but laugh.

But the Canadian guard who stood near them was growing tired of all the chatter. He stormed up to the percussionists, waving a long stick. "Shut the fuck up you two and watch the movie."

"Hey, it's only a joke," said the first percussionist, speaking in English to the Canadian.

"Yeah, he was only talking about American cocks, not Canadian ones," said the one sitting next to him in German. "I bet you Canadians have big cocks like us Germans."

The audience roared, and even some of the other Canadian guards joined in. But this guard wasn't having any of it. He poked the second percussionist in the chest with his stick, pushing him back in his seat.

The drunk soldier didn't take kindly to that and batted at the stick, trying to knock it out of the Canadian's hand. The guard reacted by bringing his other hand up to his stick and held it horizontally to strike the first percussionist across the chest, also knocking him back.

The German prisoners nearby yelled their disapproval and jumped to their feet, shouting abuse. By now, most of the Canadian guards were moving in to quell the situation. Rifles were pointed at the prisoners.

"Sit the fuck down," one guard said firmly. The Germans backed off, most returning to their seats but still shouting.

Sergeant Murray stormed over to the rows of soldiers, his rifle in his hands but not poised to shoot. "What the fuck is going on here?" he shouted.

"This fucking Kraut took a swing at me," the guard said, pointing at the drunk percussionist. The prisoner called the guard's mother a whore in German. The Canadian didn't understand it but heard the insult in his tone. They looked at each other angrily, but Neumann suspected it was all a ruse. This was the moment he had been expecting. Somehow, one or two prisoners would be separated by a guard and moved to another location where some type of exchange would take place.

Neumann looked around and saw that almost all the guards were focused on the ruckus. The movie didn't stop and the dialogue and action only added to the noise. He dropped from his seat and quickly dashed across the aisle into an outside row of seats along the theatre wall. The prisoner next to him noticed his movements, but said nothing. He quietly moved to the seat Neumann had just vacated.

The sergeant lay perfectly still on the sticky theatre floor, watching to see if any of the Canadians had noticed him. All he heard was the continuing argument between the Canadians and the Germans near the percussionist.

"Everyone shut the fuck up," he heard Murray shout again. "If you make me miss this fucking movie, I'll put the lot of you in the cooler when we get back to camp. And I'll make sure you have three shifts of KP every day till the end of the fucking war." The group quieted down. "Take these two fucking Krauts back to the truck and make them wait in the cold," Murray ordered. "When we get back, it's two weeks in the cooler for both of them. That'll teach them to act like assholes."

Neumann heard a couple of "yes Sergeant"s from the Canadians and grumbling from the two ejected prisoners.

From Neumann's point of view, they seemed to accept their fate very quickly, which further proved to him that the outburst had been planned.

Neumann peeked up and noticed that the prisoner who had taken his seat had put his arm over the back of the newly vacant one between him and his neighbour. None of the guards had noticed Neumann was no longer there. Most of the Canadians were distracted by the ruckus the two percussionists had created.

Neumann waited for a dark, nighttime scene a few seconds later to emerge from his row and crawled up the aisle on his hands and knees towards the exit to the lobby, half expecting someone to shout at him. Or even to shoot him in the back.

But he was not detected and, a moment later, he was in the lobby. It was empty. Neumann ducked behind the concession counter and waited until he heard the footsteps of the guards and two percussionists who then emerged from the auditorium.

"Move along you fucking Krauts," he heard one guard say in a voice that sounded somewhat familiar.

"No need to get rough," one of the percussionists replied. "We're out. It worked."

"Shut up. Don't talk till we get into the truck."

The front door opened, then closed. Neumann crawled to the opening at the edge of the counter and looked around. Night had set in during their time in the theatre, but the streets were well-lit and Neumann could see that the Canadians were shoving the two Germans into the back of the truck. After a moment, they glanced over their shoulders and then climbed in.

Neumann crawled quickly to the door and quietly opened it to step outside. He heard voices speaking German inside the truck and stopped in his tracks. He took a deep breath and smelled the air. It was similar to the air in the camp, yet at the same time, different. For the first time in years, he was outside, not inside a prisoner-of-war camp, on the streets of a town that was untouched by war, where no bombs were falling, and no one was shooting at him. Save for the voices in the truck, it was quiet, like those nights when he used to walk through his village, doing his rounds. If he wanted, he could start walking now and, for the length of the movie at least, no one would miss him. He could make the rounds of this town, stroll through its streets, whistling quietly, hands in his pockets, smoking a cigarette like a free man. Just for an hour or two, maybe even until sun-up, after which time he would inevitably be captured again. They'd put him in the cooler for a long time, but the feeling of being free for that short moment might be worth it. He almost pulled out a cigarette so he could start walking.

The voices in the truck suddenly got louder. "That's not enough," someone said in German. It wasn't one of the prisoners; it was a Canadian and the voice had an accent. A Tyrolian accent.

"That's all we got," said one of the prisoners in familiar German.

Neumann moved up to the back gate of the truck. He flipped the canopy aside and leaned in. "So, what have we got going on here?" he asked in German, trying to sound casual and calm.

The four men started at the sound of his voice, each one wearing a mask of horror and surprise that was illuminated by the light of an electric lantern hanging from the canvas ceiling. One of the percussionists had his shirt pulled up to reveal various items taped to his torso. Almost every inch of his chest, even around to his back, was densely covered with goods: rolls of scrip—currency that prisoners who worked in the nearby farms got paid—rolls of Canadian currency, and those small, thin boxes like the ones Neumann kept under his pillow. Inside each of those boxes, he knew, was a syrette of morphine. They would garner a lot of money on the black market.

The prisoner was a human jumble sale, a sight so strange that it was almost funny to witness. The other percussionist had opened the case to one of the drums and had punctured the head, pulling out even more goods, which the other Canadian had been putting into a kit bag.

He recognized the two Canadians. One was the Canadian with Austrian grandparents, Brunner, who he had talked with outside the hospital. He had been pulling goods off the percussionist's chest and dumping them into another large kit bag. Neumann recalled that Frank had mentioned that someone had opened a numbered account in Switzerland or Austria. Considering the guard's family ties, Neumann quickly deduced that Brunner was the one behind the account.

The other Canadian was Sergeant Hill, the guard who had escorted Neumann from the hospital's front door to the morgue. The one Sergeant Ford called a "civilian" because he had never stepped foot on the battlefield. The one who had the holster that once held the push dagger that killed Captain Schlipal.

Seeing Neumann, Hill pulled out his cudgel, his face angry.

But he was knocked aside by the panicked second percussionist. "Shit! It's Sergeant Neumann," he shouted in German, dropping his drum. He jumped up and rushed towards the gate of the truck, shoving the guard aside.

Expecting an attack, Neumann jumped back, away from the truck, letting the flap fall. But the drummer had pushed through the flap, scrambled over the gate, and started running down the street.

Neumann watched him for a few seconds, then turned when he heard the sound of someone jumping from the truck. It was Sergeant Hill with his cudgel, and he brandished it in front of him, jabbing it in Neumann's direction.

"I never got the chance to kill a Kraut in the other war, but it looks like I'll get my chance to kill one now," he said, smiling. He waved the cudgel again.

Neumann said nothing in response but did not hesitate. He rushed forward, batting the cudgel aside with the back of his right hand, the same way he rushed at an English soldier when he was taken prisoner in the Great War. That time, the soldier had held a bayonet which had given Neumann a nasty gash on his arm, so the Canadian's cudgel was nothing compared to that.

And just like he did to that English soldier in the trenches, Neumann drove his shoulder into the Canadian's stomach, roaring as he did so.

The guard grunted as the wind was knocked out of him, his body folding into Neumann.

Neumann wrapped his arms around Hill and pushed with his legs to lift the guard off the ground. They went flying backwards, smashing into the back of the truck. The whole vehicle shuddered and Neumann heard bones cracking at the impact. Neumann had tucked his head against the guard's torso to prevent it from hitting the truck, but the collision jolted him, sending a massive reverberation through his body, causing him to loosen his grip on the Canadian. Neumann fell onto his backside, his ribs bellowing in pain, and bright light flared across his vision.

For a split second, the world started to go dark but he shook it off. Neumann pushed himself to his hands and knees and rushed over to the Canadian, who lay immobile on the ground. The cudgel lay next to him, and Neumann quickly grabbed it and jumped on the guard, straddling the man's chest.

He held the weapon horizontally against Hill's neck, pressing down. In the previous war, it had been the enemy's bayoneted rifle that Neumann had slashed at the man's throat, killing him to ensure his own escape. This time it was different; Neumann did not need to escape but he did feel the need to incapacitate the Canadian. "You're not the first one to try to kill me in this war," Neumann said. "And you probably won't be the last."

"You got that right," a voice said from behind him. He recognized it as Sergeant Murray. And he also recognized the three successive clicks of a Lee-Enfield rifle being cocked. The cold metal of the barrel was pressed against his right temple.

"Tell me why I shouldn't shoot you right now," Murray said in a low, cold voice.

Neumann released the cudgel so it dropped to the ground with a clatter. He raised his hands slowly, being careful to keep his right hand away from the rifle so Murray wouldn't think he was trying to disarm him.

"They're black marketeers," Neumann said carefully in English. "Look in the truck."

Murray slowly pressed the barrel harder against Neumann's temple, stretching his neck muscles painfully as the pressure pushed his head to the side. "Look in the truck," Neumann said again.

Just then, the flap opened slightly to reveal Brunner peeking through. He took in the scene of Murray pressing a rifle against Neumann's head while the sergeant sat on his partner's chest with his hands in the air.

"Fuck," was all he said, leaning back into the truck, the flap dropping back into place.

Murray gave Neumann's head another shove with his rifle before easing up on the pressure. He lowered the gun. "Don't you fucking move, Neumann. I'm still fast enough to pull this thing up and shoot you in the head if you try anything funny."

"I'm finished with funny tonight," Neumann said, still holding his hands up.

Murray moved around him, stepping over the head of the fallen sergeant, and poked the flap of the truck canopy with his rifle. He flicked it up and pointed the weapon inside, exposing the botched exchange. Sergeant Brunner was huddled on a seat, rocking himself, while the remaining percussionist stood still with his hands in the air, shirt off, boxes of morphine still taped to his body.

"Holy Jesus," Murray said as he took in the scene. He dropped the flap around the same time a couple of the other guards came out and caught a glimpse of the men inside the truck.

"Shit Sarge, what the fuck is going on?"

Murray sighed but jerked his head towards the back of the truck. "Get those fuckers out of there and over to the jeep." The soldiers complied, opening the flap and climbing in.

"Shit, look at this," one of them said.

Murray turned to Neumann. "Fuck you, Neumann. You're a goddamn pain in my fucking ass."

A second later, he flipped his rifle around and drove the butt end of it into Neumann's cheek. There was a flash of light and pain, then darkness.

28.

Neumann slowly opened his eyes. The world spun and he felt bile rising in his throat. He shut his eyes quickly, and the spinning sensation slowed until it gradually faded away. His entire body ached with a deep soreness that penetrated every muscle and bone. There was an especially sharp pain in his cheek. For a moment, he wondered why, only to remember Sergeant Murray cursing at him. There was nothing else after that.

With his eyes still closed, he gingerly touched his cheek. He winced at the pain and felt a couple of stitches and a large bump on his face. He pulled his hand away and remained still.

He could hear little around him; the muffle of voices far away, but no words. Not even a sense of the language people were speaking. Experience told him he was in a detention cell.

He had no idea how much time had passed since the

theatre. Was it the morning after? The afternoon? Or had it already been days?

Neumann slowly opened his eyes. There was a bit of spinning, but no nausea. That was a good sign. He was also able to take in his surroundings. He had a single bed, which he was lying on, plus a latrine in a small room that was about nine square metres.

It was cold enough that he could see his breath and with his senses returning, he could now hear the wind whistling outside of the walls. He took a deep breath, closed his eyes, and sat up.

More spinning and nausea that resulted in a few dry heaves. But he forced himself to stay calm and breathe deeper until it faded. An ache formed in the back of his head. A couple minutes later, he slowly swung his legs over the side of the bed and the bout of dizziness, nausea, and deep breathing returned. He went through all that again as he stood, but he made it to the latrine without falling or wetting himself.

A sheen of sweat was clinging to his skin by the time he made it back to the bed. He was shivering so he pulled the blanket he had been lying on from underneath his body and wrapped it around his shoulders. All he could do was wait.

An indeterminate amount of time passed, time Neumann spent wondering if he had broken up Heidfeld's plan and what fallout had followed. There was the sound of footsteps outside, and they stopped in front of Neumann's door. A key sounded in the lock and the bolt moved back.

In walked Sergeant Murray looking haggard, his eyes

bloodshot as if he hadn't slept in a while. Still, the sergeant's eyes were alert. He said nothing and then stepped back out through the open door.

"It's clear. He's awake," Murray said.

"Good," said the voice of Major MacKay, who limped into the room. Neumann tried to stand at attention, but he couldn't manage to balance himself and fell back on the bed.

"No need to get up, Sergeant Neumann. I know you've had a rough time of it," the major said. "Just sit and we will dispense with the military formalities."

Right behind the major was Murray carrying a chair. He set it on the floor across from Neumann and the major sat on it. He lay his cane on his lap.

"That will be all, Sergeant," the major said. "I'll be fine here."

"Are you sure, sir?" Murray asked, giving Neumann a dirty look. "Sergeant Neumann is a dangerous man. You've seen the results from last night."

"Sergeant Neumann had his reasons for last night, which I wish to discuss with him. I'm quite sure he doesn't view me as a criminal so I'll be safe."

"I wouldn't trust him, Major. He's also a Kraut."

"Yes, I know that, but I'll be fine." He lifted his cane slightly and smiled at Neumann. "I'm also quite comfortable and adept at using my cane. And not just for walking."

Murray shot Neumann another nasty look and then saluted the major. "I'll be right outside if you need me," he said before shutting the door.

The major leaned back slightly in his chair. "So, Sergeant

Neumann, you caused a ruckus the other night with that attack against Hill. A prisoner striking a guard is a very serious offence with very serious consequences. If found guilty, we'd have no choice but to lock you up, probably for years."

"I had my reasons," Neumann said.

"Yes, and that's the only reason why you're still here and not being transferred to a military prison in Edmonton. There's a bit of leeway since the guard you attacked was a black market-eer working with enemy agents. He will serve a lot more time than you ever would. His injuries are also more severe than yours, which is why Sergeant Murray was so worried about leaving me alone with you."

"You have nothing to fear from me. You may be the enemy, but you are not a criminal. You are an honourable man, sir."

The major nodded and smiled. "And in your own way, so are you. But we've both been dealing with some dishonourable men. And before I decide whether to release you back into the camp, I need to know about Sergeant Heidfeld."

"I imagine Heidfeld has been dealt a blow that he may not recover from. He's also disappointed men on both sides who depended on him. Or decided to work with him. He'll probably stay in his hole and lick his wounds until the end of the war."

"It's a shame that many people did decide to work with him."

"This always happens, especially on the losing side. I know this from the last war. No one knows who's going to run things after it's over so they turn to someone who's confident enough to think he will." Neumann paused. "Or they were threatened. Work with him or else."

"Is that what happened to Captain Schlipal?"

Neumann stared at the major, his face impassive.

"Come on Sergeant Neumann, you must know who killed Schlipal by now."

Neumann said nothing.

"Don't be silent, Neumann. A man was killed."

"And justice will be done in some way or another. That's not my concern."

"Of course it's your concern; you're the head of Camp 133 Civil Security."

"And as head of Civil Security, it's my job to determine which soldiers have criminal intentions and to stop them. It was the same in my village: I would find the bad guys and the system—whether a judge, a magistrate, or the Führer—would determine the appropriate form of justice."

"And what justice do you think Captain Schlipal's killer will face?"

Neumann shrugged. "Military justice can take many forms. Trials and hearings, as you know. And there are other methods. Especially in war."

"Such as?"

Neumann smiled and pointed at the major's leg. "You've been in battle, Major, so you understand."

"I've only been in one battle."

"One battle is enough," Neumann replied. "Especially when

you have friends, family, and countrymen still fighting and dying in other battles."

The major seemed to fold in on himself as he quietly considered that.

"But you've been to the front lines, major, and sometimes there comes a time when someone in the battle—a comrade, a commander, or whoever—is killing or getting boys killed through their own incompetence, arrogance, or malevolence," Neumann continued. "So that person has to be removed, and that is also a form of military justice."

"More like murder, from my point of view."

"Come on, Major, you fought in Dieppe," Neumann said with a laugh. "How many Canadian boys were killed in that fiasco? Or wounded? Captured? About sixty percent, I heard." Neumann pointed at MacKay's leg. "Don't lie to me and say you don't believe someone should have been shot for planning that debacle, for allowing all those Canadian boys to be killed or captured. That would be military justice, if you ask me."

The major gripped his cane so tightly that his knuckles went white and the wood creaked. He said nothing but stared at Neumann with a look of hatred.

Neumann then smiled. "However, if you wish for some military justice that suits your temperament or your Canadian democracy, whatever that means, you might want to check the empty holster on Sergeant Hill's uniform. You'll probably discover that it matches the dagger we pulled out of Chef Schlipal."

MacKay's cane clattered to the ground.

29.

Major MacKay rushed out without saying another word. Neumann sat the edge of his bed for several moments, thinking of nothing, trying to ignore the pain in his face and waiting to see if someone would come in to release him, or to take the chair. Though he knew that the Canadians weren't the types to officially sanction the torture and beating of their prisoners—they did have some honour that way—he couldn't be sure that someone wouldn't arrange a private, "unauthorized" hearing. In his time at the camp, he had never heard nor witnessed a prisoner actually putting his hands on a Veterans Guard. Prisoners would only jeer at the guards, insult them in various ways, even pelt them with rotten produce.

There was a time in the past summer, following the death of Captain Mueller, when a large group of angry Germans almost assaulted some Canadian scouts. But Neumann had quelled the unrest by convincing the prisoners that honourable Germans wouldn't act in that manner.

But no German had actually struck a Canadian, let alone injured him to the extent that Neumann had Sergeant Hill. Neumann could argue self-defence since Hill was about to beat him with a cudgel and he was only trying to protect himself. But he knew that argument was weak. He was a German prisoner, outside the camp; it could be argued that he had been trying to escape, and since the Veterans Guards had shoot-to-kill orders, Hill was well within his rights to beat him.

Neumann knew that the clear evidence that showed that Hill and Brunner were part of a black market scheme, one that was also comprised of German prisoners, was the only reason why he was not immediately given over to the military police authorities for prosecution. MacKay also now had new evidence that directly tied a Canadian guard to the death of a German prisoner.

Still, Neumann would understand if some Veterans Guards desired to exact revenge against him, regardless of Hill's criminality. When he heard footsteps outside the room, and the sound of the door being unlocked, he pushed himself to his feet, preparing himself.

He knew he couldn't take the Canadians if they decided to punish him. He had also decided that he would not fight them; he would take the beating without lifting a hand to defend himself. Hopefully that would temper the Canadians' anger but he couldn't control that. At the very least, he would stand and face them with honour when they came.

As the door opened, he turned towards it, standing tall, impassive, at attention, the way a German soldier would when facing inspection.

Sergeant Murray stepped into the room. His face was a deep red, and although he looked momentarily surprised at the sight of Neumann standing at attention in the middle of the room, the anger quickly returned. Murray clenched his fists tightly.

He stopped a metre away from Neumann and stared at him, eyes narrowed. Neumann tried to keep his mind blank, tried to mask any animosity towards the big Canadian sergeant. And in truth, he had none. They were enemies, of course. They had probably been on the opposite sides of the battlefield in the Great War, had no doubt killed each other's countrymen and possibly even their comrades. But that was war.

And the truth was that Neumann was weary of war. And he was fairly certain the Allies were feeling the same way, despite the fact they were winning the battle. Everyone was ready to go home, to try to live with some degree of normalcy with whatever friends, family, and countrymen remained.

Neumann could see the tension building in the guard as Murray's anger rose to the surface. Neumann prepared for the strike, prepared for the beating, and for the possible arrival of other Canadians who would join in.

Yet just as Murray's anger seemed to reach its apex, he quickly turned away from Neumann, grabbed the chair, and stormed out of the room. The door closed hard behind him and locked.

30.

They kept Neumann locked behind that door for five days. He was fed and given water regularly but at no point did the Canadians allow him out of the room. He stayed in the same uniform, with only his toilet bowl as a wash basin.

Neumann didn't mind; he had gone much longer wearing the same uniform without bathing, in both this war and the previous one. And since no one was trying to kill him and he had the whole room to himself, his incarceration was a luxury when compared to some of the trenches he had lived in France and Belgium during the first war. He could see how this isolation would get to some people after a while, but he could handle it.

At no time did Major MacKay or Sergeant Murray visit him again.

On the fifth day, the door was opened by a Canadian guard

he didn't recognize. "Okay, get the fuck out, Fritz. You're free to go."

Neumann nodded. He was still in pain from the fight, but he stood up, put on his winter coat, and walked out of the cell trying his best not to show any evidence of his injuries. Two more Canadians waited outside the room and they led him down the hallway of cells and then out the main door of the detention area. The sky was spectacularly clear and blue, and Neumann was momentarily blinded by the sunlight reflected on the freshly fallen snow. The light was so bright that even though he shielded his eyes with his hand, he had to close his left eye and squint with his right.

Standing on the other side of the barbed wire fence that surrounded the detention area were Corporals Aachen and Knaup. Aachen was at ease, standing upright, looking almost like he was back to his normal self. Knaup's posture was more relaxed and he waved at Neumann.

The sergeant let a small smile come to his face and resisted the urge to wave back. "Get going," a Canadian said behind him.

The gate to the detention area was open and another Canadian was giving him an impatient look. Neumann moved forward, also noticing that there was a large group of prisoners milling about behind Aachen and Knaup.

Knaup's smile was wide when the sergeant came out on the other side of the detention gate. "It's so very good to see you, Sergeant. We were worried you'd never get out."

Neumann nodded his thanks to Knaup but addressed Aachen. "You're looking much better, Corporal."

Aachen nodded, glancing to look at Neumann's stitches and the bruising on his face. "You look like you ran into a Tiger tank."

Neumann reached up and gingerly touched his face. It still stung but not as badly as before. "Almost. But this tank was named Sergeant Murray and the thick end of his rifle."

"You mean the Canadians beat you," Knaup said with a scowl, looking to the guards in the detention centre. "That's uncalled for!" he shouted towards the Canadians.

Neumann raised a hand to quell Knaup's outburst. "No need to get angry, Corporal Knaup," he said quietly, but with some authority in his voice. "He was justified in his strike since I had thumped one of his countrymen."

Knaup turned to look at the sergeant. Aachen raised an eyebrow. "So it's true," Knaup said excitedly. "You took on the Canadians outside of the camp."

Knaup's remarks piqued the interest of many of the prisoners milling about them. Several of them cheered and gathered around the sergeant to congratulate him for his battle with the Canadians.

Neumann accepted the slaps on his shoulders and complimentary words from the prisoners with nods here and there. But he quickly became uncomfortable being the centre of attention. "I need to take a fucking shower," he said and started walking in the direction of their hut. Aachen and Knaup followed and fell into step beside him. The prisoners parted to let them go, but a group followed them as they walked. As they made their way through the camp, they continued being approached by prisoners who wanted to congratulate the sergeant for what he had done.

The attention bothered Neumann but there was little he could do to get away from it; the camp had been hit by heavy snowfall so they were forced to stick to the lattice of intersecting straight pathways that had been cleared by prisoners, making it difficult to avoid the groups of soldiers they encountered along the way.

Knaup and Aachen did their best to clear the way in front of the sergeant but it was slow going.

"Get out of the way, you fools!" Knaup shouted into the crowds. "The sergeant wants to be left alone." A few curious prisoners followed them into their hut, but Knaup herded them back outside and stood guard about three metres down from Neumann's bunk.

Aachen walked with the sergeant, watching. Neumann stopped short as he approached his bunk when he saw his viola on the bed. He turned to Aachen. "Who put that there?"

The corporal shrugged. "Don't know. I left for lunch one day and when I returned, it was sitting on your bunk. It didn't feel right to move it."

Neumann sighed, then picked up the viola and sat down on his bunk. He slid the instrument under his bed. He desperately wanted to rest, but knew that it would have to wait.

"So, what story is being told about me? About what happened outside the camp," he asked Aachen.

The corporal smiled. "There are a few versions circulating. Most say you broke up a smuggling ring between some Canadians and Germans. Others say you discovered Schlipal's killer was a Canadian and snuck outside the camp with the musicians to exact justice like some kind of masked vigilante.

"The stories all say you were attacked, some say at the concert, others say at a movie theatre, but that you fought back and defeated some Canadians, though the number of Canadians they say you bested varies; I've heard anywhere from two, to ten, to the whole city of Lethbridge."

Neumann laughed quietly. "It was only one Canadian. One who thought he was tough, but wasn't."

Aachen sat down on the empty bunk across from Neumann. "No Canadian is a match for Sergeant Neumann, is that what you are saying?"

Neumann shook his head. "That Sergeant Murray is one tough bastard," he said, pointing at his face. "And I'm pretty sure that even Major MacKay would be a tough opponent on the battlefield."

"The crippled officer?"

"Don't be so judgmental, Aachen. He may be crippled but he survived Dieppe so he must have come by that injury in battle. I'm just saying the Canadian I fought thought he was a big, tough soldier but he had never set foot on a battlefield. He had no idea what 'toughness' really meant."

"Ah, one of those," Aachen said with a nod.

"So now you know that the fight wasn't all that it's been made out to be."

"Don't worry, I won't disappoint Knaup and the others by telling the truth," Aachen replied sombrely. "We need to keep the spectre of the indomitable Sergeant Neumann alive so we can do our job with much more ease." The corporal paused and leaned forward, resting his elbows on his knees.

"What do you mean?" Neumann asked, blinking rapidly. "What's happened in the camp?"

"I'm guessing the part of the story about breaking up a smuggling ring between some Germans and Canadians is true?"

Neumann nodded.

"I thought so. Some of the musicians said as much when they returned to camp and word got around fast. It's had a big impact on the camp. Not only did you stand up to Sergeant Heidfeld and his gang, you bloodied them badly too. Many of his allies in the camp have deserted or, at the very least, are no longer afraid of him. He has lost much of his power and his threats are now meaningless."

"Where is he now?"

"No one's seen Heidfeld for a few days. He and a few of his diehard followers, like Konrad and the SS lieutenant, are hiding out in their storage building. They are so worried that they even moved some bunks in and are living there full-time. They have enough supporters guarding the place to stop anyone from coming in."

"He's afraid—but is he afraid enough to stay in there?"

"They rarely leave the place, save for meals, and only in groups of three. Even then they are jeered at and spat on by some camp members. And they always bring Heidfeld his meals. I don't think he's ever coming out."

Neumann rubbed his forehead. "I think you're right, Klaus. Or at least, I hope you're right. Heidfeld has few friends left in camp, and fewer yet outside of it. The Canadians are not happy with what he tried to do and how he corrupted some of their guards. And his civilian Canadian allies probably aren't pleased that he didn't succeed with his plan."

"So what should we do about him?"

"I don't know," Neumann said. "I think it's best if we leave him alone. He's lost most of his power, and the camp isn't afraid of him anymore. The worst thing to do to a wounded animal is to provoke it."

"The best thing to do for a wounded animal is to kill it, put it out of its misery," Aachen said plainly.

"Maybe so, but there's a good chance the Canadians will move him to another camp, one of the smaller ones in the mountains." Neumann said. "They've done that before with other troublemakers."

"So he'll get away with it."

Neumann shrugged. "Like I told Major MacKay, justice will come to Heidfeld sometime in the future, if not during the war then after. Men like him rarely last. They always go too far."

"So what do we do now?"

Neumann stood up slowly and removed his jacket. "Well, first I'm going to take a shower. And then I'm going to get something to eat. I'm fucking starving."

31.

A few days later, Neumann was lying in his bunk, huddled under his blanket for warmth, reading. Aachen had given him a Karl May novel, one starring Kara Ben Nemsi. It was an enjoyable read, exciting at times, but Neumann's experience in Africa had soured him a bit to these works. It was quite obvious that May, the most popular writer in Germany, knew nothing about life in the desert. It was described as romantic and thrilling in the novel, but nothing like the real North Africa where Neumann, Aachen, and many of the prisoners had fought for years before being captured.

Truthfully, Neumann preferred May's North American novels featuring Old Shatterhand and his Apache blood brother Winnetou. He loved those novels as a boy and carried a copy of *Old Surehand III* for a long time in the trenches of the Great War, a book he read over and over again so often that many of the pages fell out. But even with the missing pages, he would read the book again, remembering the sections that were now pressed into the dirt of the Belgian countryside.

Neumann was willing to admit to himself that after more than a year of living in Canada, he was disappointed not to have met an Apache Indian like Winnetou. No doubt there were probably a few Indians left here, but maybe they didn't live near towns; perhaps they were content to live in the wilderness like their ancestors did.

While Neumann read, he became aware of a subtle shift in the barrack's atmosphere. The air felt charged, like when a thunderstorm quickly rolled in over the landscape. He looked to his right and noticed that many of the men were talking excitedly about something and others were quickly joining in, similar to the way the infectious thrill of the hockey game had spread through the crowd the week before.

Neumann put down his book and leaned out of his bunk to look up at Aachen. The corporal had also noticed the shift in energy and was glancing around.

"Something's going on, Sergeant," he said, sitting up and swinging his legs over the edge of his bunk.

"I know," Neumann said. "I noticed it too."

Aachen had what looked to be a broken mop handle, about a metre long, in his hand. His knuckles were white from the tightness of his grip. "Do you think it's something for us to worry about?"

Neumann sat up and looked more closely at the men around him. They were excited like happy school boys at the end of a term, not like German soldiers on the eve of a battle. "If you're asking if it's Sergeant Heidfeld and his boys coming to pay us a visit, I don't think so. Something's happened. Something bigger, but not sinister."

Aachen's hand relaxed but he still held on to the stick. "Do you think the war is over?"

Neumann wasn't sure, and didn't know how he would feel about the answer. He had survived one war already and remembered the relief that came with the armistice, and the euphoria of being alive. But there was also crushing guilt that came with being lucky enough to have survived when so many millions had not. The sorrow of survival lingered with Neumann for many years, even into his second World War. It became especially keen once he had been captured and sent to Canada. And it rose up again as he wondered about the news making its way through the barracks.

The fervour of excitement rose even more as prisoners started laughing, slapping each other on the back, hugging, and pulling out contraband bottles of homemade alcohol and passing them between each other. There were even the sounds of happy crowds gathering outside, and of songs being sung.

It truly might be the end, Neumann thought.

"I think you might be right," Aachen replied, making Neumann realize that he had spoken his thoughts out loud. Aachen jumped down from his bunk and landed lightly, his injury from the summer now a distant memory. He looked out the window at the men who had gathered and were singing.

Knaup came running up to them. He was smiling and his face was flushed but bright. "Have you heard the news?" he asked. Neumann saw hope in the corporal's face; hope in response to the news but also hope that he would be the one to share it with Neumann and Aachen. The power of information was strong.

"Is the war over?" Neumann blurted. He didn't care about his abruptness; he needed to know.

"It very well could be," Knaup said. "One of the shortwave operators got a message an hour or so ago about developments on the Western Front and then another one in Hut 4, over by the west side, got a similar message. It's fantastic."

"Just tell us the goddamn news and get it over with," Aachen snapped angrily. "What's going on?"

"It's the offensive that we knew was coming," Knaup said, so happy that he didn't seem to mind Aachen's curt command. "It came in today that a couple of days ago the Führer launched a sneak attack on the Allies in the middle of the night. Took them completely unawares and we've pushed them back. Some say the Sixth Panzers are moving close to Antwerp while the Fifth and Seventh armies are heading to Brussels, splitting the Allies in half."

"That far in just two days, in the middle of winter?" Neumann asked, incredulous. "That's quite astonishing, even for the Fifth, Sixth, and Seventh armies."

"That's what caught the Allies by surprise. A big winter storm made them hunker down and ground their air support. So it's tough slogging, but once again we're pushing through the Ardennes to defeat them."

"Still, that's a long way to go in a couple of days."

"Details are still coming in but some are saying we've made it at least as far as Bastogne and have the Americans surrounded." Knaup was giddy, smiling from ear to ear and bouncing on the balls of his feet. He grabbed Aachen and shook him slightly. In the excitement of the news, Aachen didn't object. He was smiling as well.

Knaup released Aachen and left the corporal and sergeant by their bunks to go celebrate with others nearby. They greeted him joyfully, offering him a drink from one of the contraband bottles. He took a hearty swallow. After a moment, the group headed outside, happily passing the bottle between themselves, to join in the festivities.

"You think Knaup is exaggerating the action in the Ardennes?" Aachen asked. He sounded concerned but he was still smiling.

"I'm not questioning whether there was a push from us; we've been expecting it over the last few weeks. Even the Americans should have been prepared for that," Neumann said, standing up from his bunk to look out the window. "I just think it's far too soon for even the Seventh Army to have been able to push all the way to Brussels. I'm sure they and the rest of the Fifth and Sixth have been pushing, but not as far as the rumours say."

"In Stalingrad, we would hear every day that someone had broken through some line and that we were just days from taking the city," Aachen said. "But every day it was the same thing: the Russians dug in and did not let us take over."

"That's true, but don't worry, Aachen. I'm happy that

Germany has made the push but I don't think it will change much. The best we could get out of this is a negotiated peace between the Americans and Brits. And even if that happens, we've still got to deal with the Russians. They will not be open for negotiation; you of all people should know that."

Aachen nodded. "Still, it's good news. Although I worry how the Canadians will respond to all this celebration. You think we should be out there?"

"I'm too old to celebrate, Aachen, but if you wish to join the fun, I won't hold it against you."

Aachen smiled. "No, Sergeant. I was talking about us going out there and keeping an eye on things. Make sure the celebration doesn't get out of hand."

"I think it's a bit too late for that. Besides, I don't wish to be—what words did the Americans use? A 'kilroy'?—and ruin everybody's fun."

"I'm not sure that's the correct word, Sergeant."

"No matter, I don't feel like being that person. The fact we are pushing back against the Allies is a time for celebration, even if it's short-lived. And if anybody is going to ruin the fun for the rest of the camp, let it be the Canadians rather than another German."

Neumann sat back down on his bunk, picked up his novel, looked at it, then set it down. He reached underneath his mattress and pulled out a bottle of clear liquid. He removed the stopper and took a drink. The liquid burned his throat, but it was a pleasant feeling.

He sighed loudly after he swallowed, causing Aachen

to turn from the window. The corporal saw the bottle in Neumann's hand and his eyes went wide. "That's contraband, Sergeant."

Neumann took another drink. "I know. I took it off a private in Hut 6 a few months back but forgot to throw it away." He held it out to Aachen. "Unfortunately, it doesn't get better with age."

Aachen looked at the bottle, smiled, and grabbed it. He took a big sip and coughed slightly, but his face flushed and his smile grew wider.

"If you want to go out and join the younger fellows in celebration, I won't stop you. Take the bottle if you like. I have another."

Aachen shook his head. "I shouldn't be surprised by that, but I am."

"I need to keep these things for evidence," Neumann said matter-of-factly. "Or blackmail, whatever the situation demands."

Aachen took another drink and held the bottle out to Neumann. The sergeant took it and leaned back on his mattress slightly so that his head was resting on the bottom edge Aachen's bunk. He stared thoughtfully at the space in front of him, not really looking at anything. He blinked and then frowned.

"Fighting in the Ardennes in the middle of winter? Dark forest, deep snow, and our armies not sure if the clouds will hold and keep the Allied air support on the ground." He shook his head. "And the Americans. I'm sure they're surprised but they're going to dig in and try to hold the lines as much as they can. They won't want to lose any of their forward momentum from the invasion."

"If I know the Fifth, Sixth, and Seventh armies, they'll push as hard as they can, no matter the weather, no matter the odds against them," Aachen said.

"You're correct there, Corporal." Neumann took another drink, this one deep. Once the burning in his throat cleared, he turned and looked at Aachen. "I don't want to sound pessimistic, Klaus, but they are probably fighting a battle they won't win."

Aachen walked up and snatched the bottle from his hand. He took a long drink without coughing. He blew out a sharp breath and held the bottle to Neumann with a smile.

"I agree with you, August," he said, surprising the sergeant with the use of his first name. "I'd give anything to be there now. Anything to be fighting side by side with those poor bastards."

Neumann nodded and took the bottle. They finished it within the hour.

32.

Neumann woke late the next day with a pounding headache. For a moment, he wondered why he hurt so much, but then remembered the bottle of homemade brew. He also remembered the news about the Germans pushing through the Ardennes. He hoped it went well for the boys fighting through the woods, hoped they succeeded in their mission to split the Allies in two. But it was mostly a fool's hope.

The Fatherland could only push so far until the Allies would close them off. Getting to Brussels and Antwerp would be almost impossible, especially if the skies cleared and the Allies were able to send out their air support. It had been many years since Germans could match the Allies in the air; the Luftwaffe was barely a shadow of its former self.

Neumann slowly sat up in his bed, rubbing his temples. He was not averse to drinking; after all, he was a soldier with combat experience in two major wars, so he had had plenty to drink in his lifetime. And though there was an official prohibition on alcohol in the camp, there was little he could do to enforce it. Every single hut had at least one illegal still. He just made sure the brew they were making wouldn't poison anyone outright and cracked down a bit if some groups got too rambunctious when they drank.

But it had been awhile since he had drank so much; he had the headache and churning stomach to prove it. *Some food will make things better,* he thought. *Especially coffee.*

He steeled himself, swung his legs over the bed, and stood up. His vision blurred and he grabbed the bunk for balance. He closed his eyes and, after a few moments, he felt steady on his feet. He opened his eyes and they remained clear. As long as he moved slowly, he'd be fine.

Aachen's bunk was empty so he figured the corporal had gone to breakfast without him. Neumann slipped his winter coat on, stepped into his boots, and slowly trudged to the door. Many of the bunks were full, the prisoners snoring loudly, telling him that most of the camp had probably celebrated a bit too hard last night. He also had to dodge a few pools of vomit before he got to the door.

He hoped the Canadians would understand and skip this morning's count. Since the war had been going in their favour and many of the prisoners had accepted that Germany would soon lose, the guards had been a bit more lax in their schedules. They would still have counts, just not every day. And there hadn't been an escape attempt in several weeks.

Neumann knew that the even though it still officially existed, the Escape Committee rarely met. No one dug tunnels underneath huts anymore.

Outside the hut, the weather was cold, the wind biting, but Neumann welcomed it. The freshness of the winter morning helped clear his head a bit, so he breathed deep to bring more oxygen into his lungs. By the time he made it to the mess, his headache was mostly gone and the queasiness in his stomach had turned to hunger.

The mess was only half full with men scattered around at various tables. The mood in the building was subdued, no doubt due to the overconsumption of alcohol, but good-natured. Almost every prisoner was smiling as they ate or talked amongst themselves, laughing easily, but without intensity. The atmosphere was similar to the one that fell over a town a week after their team won a football championship. The more boisterous celebrations were over and an easy-going cheerfulness remained.

Because he was head of Civil Security, Neumann wasn't assigned a specific shift to eat. And since there was plenty of room in the mess due to the absence of those still sleeping off their hangovers, he chose a table by himself, off to the side. Still, there were nods of pleasant greeting from others, which he reciprocated. He exchanged a few comments about the push but the conversations were kept short. Most of the other prisoners recognized Neumann's need for food and solitude.

Because the cooks had also been out celebrating, breakfast wasn't that complicated. On his table was a bowl of toast next to a bowl of scrambled eggs. There was no meat, but he was fine with that. There were also some apples left over from the fall—a bit soft, but still edible—and a large jug of milk. More importantly, there was coffee in a covered metal pitcher. Neumann poured himself a cup and was pleased to see steam rising off of it, telling him it hadn't been sitting on the table too long. He drank it black, sipping it slowly at first.

It wasn't the best coffee he had ever had—that was in Paris—but it was a lot better than the tepid liquid they called coffee on the front lines. And a whole lot better than what anybody back home was drinking. When many of the Afrika Korps prisoners arrived in Camp 133, a good number of them refused to eat some of the wonderful food the Canadians had provided for them. They thought it would be disloyal to eat so well while others still on the lines or back home did not.

But that attitude faded over time as they gave into the temptation, and Command issued a directive saying that it was important for the prisoners to stay well fed so when the time came for them to fight, they would be strong. It had been a long time since anyone in the camp actually thought they would fight again.

Neumann finished half a cup of coffee, feeling instantly more awake, and then scooped some eggs into a bowl, adding a couple of pieces of toast on the side. He ate slowly so as not to upset his stomach. But as he continued to eat, the queasiness disappeared and his energy started to rise. He wasn't operating at one hundred percent, but the hangover was much diminished.

He was just starting his third cup of coffee and his second

round of eggs and toast when Aachen entered the mess and approached him. "Corporal Aachen, it's good to see—" he started to say with a bright smile. But the look on the corporal's face stopped him mid-sentence. Aachen's face was white, not because of a hangover or sickness, but something else. There was deep sadness in his eyes.

"What happened?" Neumann asked.

Aachen blinked back tears, creating a sense of dread in the sergeant's stomach. "You have to come with me," Aachen said plainly.

"What's going on, Corporal?"

"You have to come, Sergeant," Aachen said, his voice catching. "Now." Aachen didn't wait for Neumann's response; he turned quickly and headed towards the front door of the mess. Several prisoners watched him go and whispered amongst themselves, wondering what was going on.

Neumann didn't hesitate. He left his coffee and food behind and followed Aachen, putting on his coat as he did so.

Neumann caught up with Aachen at the door, which he held open for the sergeant. "Where are we going, Corporal?"

"To the hospital," Aachen said. For a second, he looked almost ready to break down but he quickly gathered his composure. "It's Knaup."

"What about him?" Neumann demanded. "What's happened to Knaup?"

Aachen tried to speak but his voice had left him. After a few seconds and a hard swallow, he said, "You'll have to see."

33.

They both ran through the snow and cold, ignoring calls
from prisoners asking why they were in a hurry. Neumann
braced himself for the worst but couldn't understand what
could have happened to Knaup. Last time they saw him, the
corporal was having a good time, laughing and celebrating
with the other prisoners. What harm could have befallen him?

These thoughts and others ran through Neumann's mind as
they ran to the hospital. Once inside, he didn't remove his wet
boots or his coat. He let Aachen led him to Knaup. Neumann
breathed a sigh of relief when they headed away from the
morgue, but that relief vanished when Aachen ushered him
into a room and he saw what was there.

Knaup was in a bed, attached to a series of tubes that snaked
from glass bottles of clear liquid. Neumann couldn't see where the
lines connected to Knaup's body because the corporal was covered

by a blanket. Only Knaup's face was exposed but the skin was grey, like a dead man's. Neumann's heart fell at the sight of the boy.

Doctor Kleinjeld was standing by the side of the bed, adjusting one of the bottles. An orderly stood next to the doctor. Neumann rushed to the bedside.

"Is he alive?" Neumann asked, almost breathless with shock and fear.

Kleinjeld nodded, but slowly. "For now, but he's in a coma and I'm not sure he'll come out."

"What happened to him?" Neumann asked.

"Alcohol poisoning."

"Alcohol poisoning?" Neumann almost shouted.

The doctor nodded. "Unfortunately, he's not my only case today. Some of the prisoners' celebrations got a bit out of hand last night, drinking that horrible brew that some people cook up. Most of my cases were minor, but Corporal Knaup here is my worst case."

"Will he recover?"

Kleinjeld paused before answering. "I wish I could say 'yes,' but I really have no idea. He's in a coma and we're doing our best to rehydrate him and clear his system but it might be too late. It's a good thing Sergeant Olster found him when he did."

"Olster," Neumann said, looking around the room. He had been so shocked and focused on Knaup that he didn't notice who else was in the room with them. Seated in the corner was Sergeant Olster, a bit worse for wear, but still looking hard and angry. Next to Olster was Corporal Tenefelde, whom it took Neumann a moment to recognize.

"I found him by one of the classrooms." Olster said, standing up and stepping forward. "I heard some celebrations last night but didn't go out into the yard in case someone decided to take advantage of the situation and attack me. So I stayed in the wrestling room for most of it. But then I heard some voices come near and thud on the ground near the window. Then the voices left. I decided to see what was going on and I found Knaup in the snow, smelling of booze. I thought he was dead, but there was a bit of a heartbeat. So I grabbed him and tried to carry him to the hospital. Tenefelde saw me and jumped in to help."

"I thought he was carrying someone as a kind of joke," Tenefelde said. "But then he said we had to get to the fucking hospital." Tenefelde flushed and looked around. "I didn't know it was Knaup until we got him here."

"They probably saved his life, at least for the moment," Kleinjeld said. "If he had been left there, his body would have shut down and he would have died. Even so, he's still in grave danger because the alcohol is still in his system. We're doing what we can, but he has an acute liver injury which could cause some serious damage to his brain and the rest of his body. All we can do now is wait."

Neumann shook his head and sat down heavily on the chair next to the bed. "I can't believe Knaup would drink so much."

"I'm not sure it was entirely his fault," Aachen said quietly.

Neumann looked at him. "What are you talking about, Corporal?"

Aachen glanced over at Tenefelde. Tenefelde hesitated so

Olster gave him a hard elbow in the ribs. He winced in pain, but quickly recovered.

"When I found Sergeant Olster carrying Knaup, I went over to help," Tenefelde said slowly. "So we worked to carry Knaup together but when we moved him, something fell out of his pocket. Something small, but it was shiny in the light. Olster said we should leave it but I picked it up anyway. When I picked it up, I knew exactly what it was."

"What was it?" Neumann asked, rising to his feet. "Give it to me."

Tenefelde hesitated again and Olster pushed him forward. Tenefelde dug in his pocket and held the object out to the sergeant. Neumann stared at it. It was a small syrette, just like the one Neumann had under his pillow. Just like all the ones taped to the German musician in the truck.

"I couldn't figure out why Knaup had it," Tenefelde said. "Because he didn't have any injuries that required morphine."

Neumann reached out and took the syrette from Tenefelde's hand. He held it in his palm, feeling the weight of the object. His anger began to rise as he looked between the drug and Knaup, lying there, almost dead. He knew that Knaup wouldn't have consciously drank himself into this state. Someone forced him to do so, hoping to kill him. And by leaving the syrette in Knaup's pocket, he was leaving a message.

It was Heidfeld, getting back at Neumann for ruining the exchange of money and morphine in Lethbridge after the concert. Heidfeld didn't have the guts to face Neumann head-on, but went after someone close to him instead.

Neumann's anger boiled over but he didn't know if he was angrier at Heidfeld or at himself for not believing that the man would strike back.

"FUCK!" he screamed, throwing the syrette to the ground and smashing it beneath his boot.

34.

"See here, Sergeant Neumann!" doctor Kleinjeld exclaimed. "That kind of action is uncalled for."

Neumann whirled on the doctor. "Get the fuck out of here, Doctor Kleinjeld," he said, his hands clenched into fists. The orderly turned white with fear and quickly ran out of the room. The doctor did not.

"Who do you think you are, Sergeant Neumann? This is my hospital and I decide—"

Corporal Aachen interrupted the doctor by putting a hand on his shoulder, squeezing slightly. "It would be best if you leave now, Doctor," he said quietly.

Kleinjeld took a quick glance at Aachen, then at Neumann. He opened his mouth to speak but thought better of it when he saw how angry Neumann was. He brushed at Aachen's hand and the corporal removed it from his shoulder. Kleinjeld pulled down on his smock to adjust it and then turned slowly on his heel. Before he left the room, he turned to address Aachen. "If he breaks anything of value in this room," he said, pointing at the sergeant, "I will hold you personally responsible, Corporal."

Aachen nodded. The doctor left the room and shut the door.

Neumann looked over at Tenefelde, who was shaking slightly. "Block the door, Corporal Tenefelde," he barked. Tenefelde instinctively stiffened at the tone of Neumann's voice. Olster did the same; suddenly, the two of them were no longer just prisoners of war, but soldiers waiting for orders. Tenefelde quickly walked over to the door and stood in front of it, facing the room.

Neumann nodded at him. Then all the angry tension left his body. He sat down on the edge of Knaup's bed as if he was deflating and rubbed his face with his right hand.

"Fuck," he said.

Aachen walked up to the sergeant, close enough to touch him, but he didn't. "You had no idea this would happen."

"I should have expected something like this from Heidfeld," Neumann said, still rubbing his face. "I pushed him into a corner and, like a cornered animal, he lashed back. Unfortunately, it was Corporal Knaup who took the brunt of my stupidity while I was getting drunk."

"We all got drunk, Sergeant," Aachen said.

"Of course we did," Tenefelde blurted out. "Germany won a great victory."

All the other prisoners in the room, except Neumann, turned quickly to Tenefelde and gave him an angry look. Neumann looked at him sadly. "It's only a temporary victory, Corporal. That's all. We've bloodied the Allies a little bit, but like Heidfeld, they'll strike back. People we care about will die and Germany will lose another war."

The tone of his voice tempered all the anger in the room. The soldiers shifted uneasily and looked away from each other, staring at the floor or a spot on the wall instead.

"So we just give up?" Tenefelde asked after a while.

"There's no way we can beat the Allies, you shithead," Olster said. "The Yanks and the Brits will push through the Western Front while the fucking Ivans burn and loot through the east. Best to give up now and prevent a bloodbath."

"That's not what I'm talking about," Tenefelde said.

"Then what the fuck are you talking about?" Olster growled.

"Hold on," Aachen said, walking over to Tenefelde and pointing at him. "Chris has a point."

"No, he doesn't. He's an idiot," Olster said.

"Shut up you two," Neumann snapped. Olster and Tenefelde jerked to attention again. Neumann then turned to Aachen. "It's not a good idea, Klaus. We tried to do this before and look what happened to Knaup."

"That's because we tried to play his game. We tried to think like a criminal and cut him off from his money and supplies when we should have been thinking differently."

"There's too many of them," Olster said, finally understanding. "We'll get killed."

"So what if we do?" Aachen replied. "We're German soldiers in the middle of a war. If we die in battle against the enemy, then we die as honourable Germans."

"But they're Germans, too," Tenefelde said. "They aren't the enemy."

"Of course they are," Aachen retorted. He gestured between himself and Neumann. "Knaup was part of our squad and they all but killed him. They may be German, but they killed one of our own because they wanted to protect their criminal interests." Aachen took a deep breath walked over to Olster. "Just like those cowards who tried to kill you," Aachen said. "Just like those cowards who tried to assassinate the Führer."

Olster's face hardened. Aachen nodded at him. "Those who tried to assassinate the Führer were Germans. Germans considered loyal enough to be invited to a meeting with the Führer. But they weren't. They were traitors with a secret bomb that killed other loyal and honourable Germans for their own ends, not Germany's. Just like Sergeant Heidfeld. He claims to look out for the future of Germany, but he's only in it for himself.

"And Heidfeld was responsible for this," Aachen turned to point at Knaup. "For harming this honourable German who was my friend. That makes them the enemy in my eyes. And in a time of war, we must fight the enemy. Or die trying."

Aachen looked over at Tenefelde, who gave him a firm nod. He turned back to Olster who was turning red with anger. "Fucker deserves to die," Olster said through clenched teeth.

They all looked to Neumann, who had been watching

Aachen's passionate speech. He laid his hand on the sheet that covered Knaup's body. Then he nodded and stood up.

Aachen, Tenefelde, and Olster all faced the sergeant and stood at attention, awaiting instruction.

"Okay, if we're going to do this, I need to know one thing," Neumann said quietly. "Who are the toughest sons of bitches in this fucking war?"

There was a pause. Tenefelde and Olster looked at each other. "Afrika Korps?" Tenefelde said tentatively.

Olster nodded. "Yeah, the fucking Afrika Korps."

Then they both proudly shouted, "Afrika Korps!"

Neumann nodded and looked over at Aachen. They smiled. "Nice sentiment boys," Neumann said. "But this isn't a pep talk. If we're going to fight Heidfeld and his platoon, we're going to have to be tougher than Afrika Korps were in the desert."

"But Afrika Korps *are* the toughest sons a bitches in the war," Tenefelde said. "Everyone in the camp knows that."

"That's because almost everyone in the camp came from Afrika Korps," Neumann said. "But the reason we are in this camp is because we lost to the Tommies and the Yanks. Because we underestimated them, and were taken prisoner. So Africa Korps *was* tough, but not as tough as we thought we were."

"So the Brits and the Yanks are the toughest?" Olster asked, incredulous. "With all due respect, Sergeant, fuck that. Montgomery is a shit cripple and the son of a whore."

"I agree with that, Olster," Neumann said. "But even

though the Brits and Yanks beat us in Africa, they aren't that tough."

"The Canadians, then?" Tenefelde guessed again.

Neumann shook his head. "Tough, but not the toughest." He pointed at Aachen. "Corporal Aachen knows the answer, don't you Klaus?" Aachen nodded.

Neumann continued. "He knows who the toughest sons of bitches are in this war because he is the only one in this room, possibly in the whole camp, who fought against those bastards. His stories about them make everything I've seen in *both* wars seem like a birthday party."

Tenefelde and Olster looked over at Aachen, their expressions questioning.

"The Ivans," Aachen said.

"The Ivans," Neumann repeated with a nod.

"The fucking Russians are assholes," Olster said. "They don't fight like regular people; they fight like blood-crazed animals."

"That's exactly right," Aachen agreed.

Neumann took a step forward. "The Ivans run into battle unarmed so they can kill a German with their bare hands and take his weapon. They take no prisoners, and they'd kill the dead a second time if they could. They will burn and loot across all of Eastern Europe to kill as many Germans as possible before this war is over."

Olster and Tenefelde looked at each other, confused. "So what the fuck is that supposed to mean, Sergeant?" Olster said.

"It means, Sergeant Olster, that when we go against Heidfeld and his ilk, we will not act like honourable German soldiers;

we will fight like the fucking Ivans. We will show them no mercy, even if they belong to the Waffen SS. We will not be afraid of those fuckers and will use them as an example. The whole camp will know that nobody fucks with the members of my squad, because if they do, they will pay the same price."

35.

Konrad came out of the north door of Mess #3 picking his teeth with a toothpick. He was flanked by two prisoners whom Neumann did not recognize. They were a bit taller than the Waffen SS sergeant, but thinner. Konrad looked up at the sky, shivered a bit, and then pulled the lapels of his jacket together, trying to close it further; his sizeable gut prevented that.

Neumann, along with Aachen, Olster, Tenefelde, and Wissman, who had since joined them, stood near the steps on the first barracks north of the mess. As soon as Konrad and the other two soldiers started walking, Neumann moved forward. Aachen and the other three followed right behind him. Olster took a couple more puffs on the cigarette he had been smoking and then tossed it into the snow. He trailed behind the group, but quickly caught up.

Konrad didn't notice them until they were about three metres away. He chuckled slightly when he saw Neumann and his group striding towards him with purpose, but he didn't stop walking. He gave Neumann a disdainful smile. His companions, though, exchanged worried glances and slowed slightly, allowing Konrad to be about a step and a half ahead of them.

Both groups met about halfway between the two buildings, and stopped. Neumann paid no attention to Konrad's companions and locked eyes with the other sergeant. Konrad gave a quick glance at the group in front of him before he met Neumann's gaze.

"This is all you brought to deal with me, with us?" he said. He pulled the toothpick out of his mouth and flicked it at Neumann. It bounced off Neumann's coat and into the snow.

Neumann didn't flinch but Tenefelde looked ready to attack Konrad for his insolence. Wissman placed his hand on Tenefelde's chest, holding him back. Instead, Tenefelde spat at the ground near Konrad's feet.

Konrad shot Tenefelde a venomous look before turning back to address Neumann. "You seem to be losing the discipline of your men, Sergeant Neumann. But that's typical of the Wehrmacht. No discipline. The Waffen SS is a completely different story." Konrad pointed at the two men flanking him, who were looking around with growing concern, especially as more prisoners noticed what was going on and started to gather around.

Neumann looked over at the prisoner on the right of Konrad, then to the one on the left.

"Go," was all he said.

Konrad chuckled. But the two men looked at each other, nodded slightly, and left, both heading in opposite directions. Konrad looked left then right, frowning as he watched his supporters leave him. He took a deep breath and turned back to face Neumann.

"No matter, Neumann. You can try to take me, but I will put up a great fight, even against your little group here," he said. He swung his arm in a half circle to point at the gathering group of prisoners around them. "Even if *all* of you try to take me, you will learn that Sergeant Eduard Konrad does not go down easy. I will fight and you might win, but you will all pay a great price."

Neumann opened his mouth to respond but stopped when Corporal Aachen stepped up to the Waffen SS sergeant. "I will fight you alone, Sergeant Konrad," Aachen said. "There will be no need for anyone else to step in."

Konrad laughed, looking down at Aachen. The corporal was about a head shorter than Konrad, but they had a similar stature; however, where Konrad was mostly fat, Aachen was muscle. Still, it was obvious that Konrad had some strength.

"You want payback for what I did to you in the shower last summer, do you, boy?" Konrad said. "Again, that shows a typical lack of Wehrmacht discipline, thinking of revenge. It weakens you."

"I've found that revenge makes one stronger," Aachen said. "Gives you more heart in a fight."

"Ha! We will find out," Konrad said, shrugging his shoulders dramatically to remove his winter coat. He rolled up his sweater sleeves to the elbow. "No wrestling, but a good old-fashioned fistfight between titans." He raised his fists like a boxer, planted his feet, and tossed a couple of shadow punches in Aachen's direction. His punches were fast and whistled slightly as they cut through the air. His hands looked like gigantic hams.

Aachen said nothing for a moment, then turned, removing his winter jacket. He handed it to Tenefelde, who draped it over his own arm. They repeated the motions with his sweater.

Neumann leaned over as Aachen removed another shirt and handed it to Tenefelde. "Are you sure about this, Corporal?" he asked softly.

Aachen responded with a curt nod. He had stripped down to his sleeveless undershirt and although it was about -5 °C, if he felt the cold, he didn't show it. He turned to face Konrad, who was smiling.

"I was the heavyweight champion of my battalion," said the Waffen SS sergeant. "Almost killed the last person I fought."

Aachen raised his fists and nodded. "I was that man you tried to kill in the shower. And there were six of you and only one of me. And you still failed."

Konrad blinked once at that, but then shook it off. "So be it."

He attacked first, his feet shuffling forward quickly, much faster than anyone expected for such a big man. He jabbed with his left hand, a shot that Aachen easily batted away with his right. Konrad followed that one up with powerful round-house with his right. Aachen leaned away from the blow, but it still glanced off the side of his head. He froze for a second, almost as if he was stunned by the hit.

Konrad smiled and threw another left, coming in for the other side of Aachen's head. But something seemed to click inside of Aachen. The corporal immediately stepped inside the larger man's reach. He threw three punches in all. The first was a sharp right jab to Konrad's solar plexus. The Waffen SS sergeant exhaled sharply from the power of the blow, his mouth opening wide and his tongue flapping. His eyes went wide. Aachen's second blow struck, a swift but solid left hook that caught Konrad on the side of his head. His neck snapped sideways and a tooth flew out of his mouth, flowed by a stream of blood. This shot was immediately followed by a fierce right uppercut that connected with the bottom of Konrad's chin. His head snapped up and back. The blood was flowing as Konrad's chin and four of Aachen's knuckles all split at the impact.

Aachen deftly danced back as Konrad crumpled into a heap on the pathway. A cloud of snow rose up around the sergeant as he landed, hard, and then slowly settled on him.

The fight lasted less than five seconds and the crowd stared at Konrad in stunned silence as Aachen turned to grab a shirt hanging from Tenefelde's arm and started putting it on.

And then there was a great cheer from the crowd. A couple of prisoners bent down to look at Konrad to see if he was alive. Neumann was about to say something to Aachen but Olster pushed the sergeant aside and grabbed Aachen by the shoulders, shaking him.

"Holy fuck you little bastard! You knocked him on his ass before he even had a chance to blink," Olster said, almost laughing. "You're a much better boxer than a wrestler."

"My older brother was a boxer," Aachen said, accepting Olster's compliments. "I had to learn to battle with him in order to survive."

"Then hats off to your brother because that was the best bit of boxing I've seen in a while." Olster shook him again before releasing him. He walked over to the unconscious Konrad and spat at his feet.

"This is what happens if you're an asshole and a criminal who works with our enemies," Olster shouted at the crowd. "Sergeant Neumann did it to the Canadians for what they did to Schlipal, and Corporal Aachen has just shown you again what will happen if you try to threaten or kill your way into power or money in the camp. If you fuck with us—with Sergeant Neumann and his squad in this camp— this will be you." Olster pointed and then spat again at the fallen Konrad.

The crowd cheered and began to chant Neumann's and Aachen's names.

Olster smiled and turned to Neumann, who was looking a bit uncomfortable with the speech and the response from the crowd. But the sergeant said nothing.

"What the fuck should we do with this asshole, Neumann?" Olster asked.

For the first time since the fight started, Neumann spoke. "Take him to the legionnaire hut."

Olster, Tenefelde, and some of the other prisoners stiffened at Neumann's statement. "The legionnaire hut, Sergeant? Are you sure that's wise?" Tenefelde asked. Aachen was still taking clothes from his outstretched arm and getting dressed.

"They'll be expecting him. They are our German allies in this, as they have always been," Neumann said, again generating a shock wave of surprise through many of the prisoners. Neumann waved his hand at Olster and the two soldiers who were bent down looking at Konrad. "You heard me! Get him to the legionnaire hut," he shouted.

They nodded and quickly scrambled to lift Konrad. It wasn't easy because the Waffen SS sergeant was big and mostly dead weight. A few other prisoners pitched in and they managed to lift Konrad up by carrying him the way a group of trophy hunters would carry a lion or gorilla after it was shot. The group that had gathered for the fight decided to follow those that carried Konrad. "And get Dr. Kleinjeld to have a look at him," Neumann shouted after them.

Someone shouted back in the affirmative so Neumann turned back to Aachen. The corporal was just pulling on his sweater.

"I didn't know you had an older brother," Neumann said. "You never once mentioned him."

"You never told me you played the viola," Aachen retorted. Then he took a deep breath. "He died in 1939. It happened so long ago—it feels like a hundred lifetimes have passed since then—and I sometimes forget. It was only when Konrad threw that first punch that I remembered, that I thought it was my brother who was trying to hit me. I balked, just enough for Konrad to clip me with his second punch, but it was enough to snap me out of it and realize that it wasn't him, that it will never be him again. Then I got angry, and … well, you saw the result of that."

"Konrad had it coming to him," Tenefelde said. "And you did say we should show no mercy so I figured that's what you were doing."

"I guess you're right. But I do miss my brother," Aachen said.

"And I miss my cousin," Wissman added. "And all those lads I served with who weren't as lucky as me."

"Like Knaup," Tenefelde added.

Neumann and Aachen quickly turned towards Tenefelde. Wissman slapped him across the shoulder. "You idiot," he said, raising his hand to strike again.

Aachen stepped in and grabbed his wrist to stop him. "Tenefelde's right. I miss Knaup. We should all be thinking of him because that's why we're doing this." Aachen released his hold on Wissman, who quickly backed away.

The corporal shrugged, grabbed his coat from Tenefelde, and slipped it on, pulling it tightly around him and zipping it up. He flexed the fingers of his right hand, wincing as the splits in his knuckles opened and closed.

"Let's go get the next one."

36.

Neumann, followed by Aachen, Tenefelde, and Wissman, strode into the administration building. They marched with determination, their boots thumping against the floor, announcing their presence to everyone in the building but also stating that they would broker no opposition.

Several prisoners carrying papers in the hallway quickly clutched their documents to their chests and moved out of the way to let them pass. Several others looked up from their desks or stuck their heads out their doors to see what the commotion was all about. Some dashed back into their rooms when they saw it was Neumann and his group, while others watched with incredulity as they passed by.

The eyes of the onlookers widened and whispers were tossed back and forth between administrators when Neumann and the group turned into the office of the SS lieutenant.

They filed into the office one at a time, stomped one heel to the ground in unison, and snapped to attention. They all raised their arms in the straight-arm salute and shouted, "Heil Hitler!"

If the SS lieutenant was surprised by the group's sudden and thunderous entrance into his office, he didn't show it. He looked up from his papers, taking off his glasses as he did so. He raised his hand in salute and responded with his own, but quieter, "Heil Hitler."

For a moment, he stared at the group standing in front of him, saying nothing. They responded in kind; Neumann was following strict protocol by not speaking to an officer until he was spoken to.

"Sergeant Neumann?" the lieutenant asked. "What is the meaning—"

Neumann didn't let him finish. The lieutenant's words had fulfilled protocol so there was no need to continue the pretense of respect.

"You are under arrest, Lieutenant, so you must come with me," Neumann said. He gestured to Aachen and Tenefelde who both moved to flank the lieutenant on opposite sides of his desk.

"You cannot be serious, Sergeant Neumann." He stood tall and stiff in an attempt to use his standing and rank to intimidate. "You are making a major mistake."

"As the head of Civil Security of Camp 133, under the authority of the Führer, Adolph Hitler, Supreme Commander of Armed Forces of the Great German Reich, I charge you with crimes against the Wehrmacht and the German people. The first charge is theft and misappropriation of military property, the second is unauthorized use of government property—"

"This is preposterous, Sergeant Neumann. I will not stand for such accusations."

Neumann continued as if the lieutenant said nothing.

"Collusion with others in order to steal military property; committing fraud against the German military and people in order to personally profit; collusion with others in order to commit fraud against the German military and people in order to personally profit. All these charges were committed during a time of war, which further adds to their seriousness."

Aachen and Tenefelde came around the desk from opposite sides and attempted to put their hands on the lieutenant. He shook them off and raised a fist of defiance. "I will not stand for this. *Command* will not stand for this. And believe me when I say that there are those in Berlin who will be contacted and who *will not stand for this.* You are in big trouble, Neumann. Trouble you do not want. Not for you, or for your men here."

Neumann continued, looking at the lieutenant with narrowing eyes. "Collusion with the enemy during a time of war; collaborating with the enemy during a time of war; and, finally, because of the charges of collusion and collaboration with the enemy, treason against the Great German Reich, its peoples, and the Führer."

The lieutenant turned to Aachen. "Corporal, if you leave now, I will spare you. I will say that you only followed the orders of your commander and, thus, are blameless in this. However, if you remain, it will not go well for you. Or for your family in Germany; your mother and your father will suffer your consequences the same way family members of those traitors who tried to kill the Führer suffered." He turned to Tenefelde. "The same goes for you, Corporal Tenefelde; leave now or your sister and her children in Trier will suffer. They will—"

Neumann rushed at the lieutenant's desk and, grabbing it by the corner, heaved it against the wall. It toppled over with a crash and the drawers flew open to spew their contents on the floor. Tenefelde had to quickly step aside to dodge some of the heavier falling objects. The sudden sound of the crash echoing through the office and down the halls into the administrative building silenced the lieutenant for a moment.

Neumann stepped into the now-empty space between himself and the SS lieutenant. "This is unnecessary—" the lieutenant started to say, fear now rising in his eyes.

Neumann backhanded the lieutenant across the face with his left hand, the smack echoing almost as loudly as the crashing desk. The lieutenant staggered to the left but was caught by Tenefelde. The corporal brought the SS lieutenant to a standing position and Neumann hit him again, swinging his same hand to land an open-handed slap across his face.

Aachen caught the lieutenant this time and brought the SS officer back to his feet. Neumann did not strike a third time. Instead, he grabbed the lieutenant by his collar and pulled his face close, just inches from his own. The lieutenant's eyes were wide with fear, and he was almost to the point of tears.

"You have no right to speak," Neumann hissed angrily. "You have committed acts of treason during a time of war against the Wehrmacht, the German people, and the Führer. You are a traitor and will be tried, judged, and punished in the manner befitting a traitor."

"What is the meaning of this?" a voice spoke from the door.

Tenefelde and Aachen immediately let go of the lieutenant and snapped to attention, saluting. The SS officer almost fell but caught himself and managed a salute.

Neumann slowly turned, then moved to attention and saluted as well. "General Varnhagen," he said.

Standing in the door was the German commander of the camp. General Varnhagen was a few years older than Neumann—just under fifty, relatively young for a general—but was one of Rommel's confidantes during the battles in North Africa. He was trim and his short black hair was combed back along his scalp. He wore a pair of round wire-rimmed glasses and his uniform was impeccable. He carried a riding crop in his left hand. It was an affectation that many did not like, but Varnhagen had the respect of many of the men. When it was certain that North Africa would fall to the Allies, many generals and their aides decided to flee to Europe. Varnhagen was invited by Rommel to do the same, but he insisted that some higher-ranking officers should remain behind to be captured as a good example for the rest of the men. It was said that the Desert Fox kissed Varnhagen on both cheeks when he made that statement.

"What is all this noise, Sergeant Neumann? What are you doing to the lieutenant?"

The SS officer took a step forward to address Varnhagen. "General, Sergeant Neumann was—"

"I was not asking you, Lieutenant," Varnhagen snapped. "I was asking Sergeant Neumann."

The lieutenant bit his tongue and stepped back between Aachen and Tenefelde.

"General, forgive our intrusion into your building," Neumann said. "However, I am acting in my role as head of Civil Security to arrest the lieutenant for crimes of collusion with the enemy and treason, amongst other things. He resisted and I was called upon to make him understand the seriousness of these crimes."

"Those are serious allegations, Sergeant Neumann, especially for someone like the lieutenant. I hope you understand the significance of what you are doing."

"I am well aware of it, General. I'm aware of the lieutenant's standing in our military. However, he has gotten himself involved with certain members of our camp who have engaged in various crimes such as misappropriation of goods, gambling, black marketeering, and collusion with Canadians outside the camp. These people have amassed some power in the camp, have threatened many prisoners during these activities, and may have been involved in the death of Captain Schlipal."

Varnhagen's eyes widened at that. "I had a long talk with

Major MacKay from the Veterans Guards about your actions. He was not pleased that a German prisoner left camp to take matters in his own hands, and neither was I; it was a most reckless action on your part, Sergeant."

Neumann nodded. "I'm sorry if it caused you grief with the Canadians."

"I'm not entirely sure you mean that, Neumann, but you've always been one who gets results, especially in battle. Even Rommel himself mentioned you once or twice during briefings."

Neumann blinked, surprised to hear that the Desert Fox actually knew who he was. He was speechless.

"Despite the expressions of displeasure and frustration from Major MacKay, he was unable to hide a grudging respect for your actions. You did assist him in apprehending two of his own guards who were in collusion with the enemy."

Varnhagen looked over Neumann's shoulder at the SS lieutenant. "And you are saying this lieutenant is involved in the same scheme?"

Neumann nodded.

The general nodded back but then leaned in close to Neumann. "Are you sure about this, August? Are you sure you wish to take this step and arrest this Waffen SS officer?"

Neumann nodded. "Yes, General. I believe this action is necessary to help break this criminal ring."

"I've been aware of their schemes for some time but uncertain of the best course of action to deal with them," Varnhagen said, speaking softly so only Neumann could hear him. "Or how to get rid of the SS asshole without pissing someone off."

"These kinds of groups are difficult because they tend to resurrect themselves before too long," Neumann whispered back. "But I've learned if you cut off the heads, the rest of the body quickly dies."

"I expect a report about this on my desk once you're done. And it better be an air-tight case."

"Yes, sir."

The general nodded and then stepped back. "Okay, Neumann. You have shown time and time again that you are the best man to be our head of Civil Security, that you have the best interests of the men in camp in mind," General Varnhagen said loudly, so anyone within earshot, both inside and outside the room, would hear. "I trust your judgment on this, so please, proceed."

The SS lieutenant's legs gave out beneath him but Aachen and Tenefelde grabbed him before he fell. Neumann saluted the general as he left the office and then turned around. "Take this piece of shit out of here," Neumann said, pointing at the lieutenant. "He will be dealt with later."

Aachen and Tenefelde started to frog-march him out of the office. The lieutenant shouted some remarks about injustice and made threats, but Neumann slapped him. "Shut the fuck up or I'll knock you out."

The lieutenant went silent, save for some curses under his breath. He struggled against Aachen and Tenefelde but they held him tight.

At the door, Aachen turned to the sergeant. "To the legion-naires' hut, Sergeant?"

Neumann nodded. "For the time being. We'll deal with him later."

Aachen nodded and started to move away. "Aachen," Neumann called after him "I want you to stay with him. Until you hear differently."

Aachen raised his eyebrows. "Are you sure, Sergeant?"

"That's an order, Corporal."

Another raise of the eyebrows from Aachen. Neumann nodded. "I'm confident I can handle Staff Sergeant Heidfeld by myself."

"So you say," Aachen said dubiously.

"After word gets around about this," Neumann said, pointing to the grumbling SS lieutenant, "no one will stay with Heidfeld now. He will be alone. There is no need to worry."

"There is always a need to worry, Sergeant. That's my job in your squad. But if you say you can handle it and order me to let you go, there is nothing I can do."

"Your concern is noted, Corporal Aachen, as it always is," Neumann said. "But I can handle it."

"Yes, Sergeant," Aachen said with a quick nod. He motioned to Tenefelde and the two men hauled the SS lieutenant from the room.

"Neumann!" he cried, "Neumann! Don't do this to me."

His shouts and sobs faded as he left the building. Neumann knew that the sight of Aachen and Tenefelde dragging the SS lieutenant through the administrative building and the camp would attract attention. So would General Varnhagen's support of the arrest. And that's exactly what he wanted. The symbolic gestures were important for the prisoners to see.

Neumann did not follow them to watch the spectacle. He did not even leave the office. He turned away from the door and sat down on the SS lieutenant's chair and waited. Waited for the news to spread in the camp, waited for Heidfeld to realize that he was now alone. Waited for nightfall and his chance to confront the staff sergeant.

37.

Neumann quietly entered the classroom building. He listened carefully, moved in slowly and his body was tense but poised to respond in case Heidfeld decided to ambush him. The odds were against that, but he figured it was best to be prepared for the unexpected. Heidfeld probably knew he was alone, probably knew that someone was going to come for him soon, be it Neumann, the Canadians, or someone else, so he might be desperate. But Heidfeld wasn't a true combat veteran. He had served in a war zone, but only as an adjutant to a higher-ranking officer. He had the training for combat, been shelled by enemy artillery, and been under air attack from time to time, but never fought in direct contact with the enemy. Despite his bluster and his threats to various people in the camp, he had never directly killed someone in the war. That was a task he appointed to his minions, and Neumann had already dealt with those. He would make short work of the staff sergeant as well.

There was no ambush, just a quiet hallway. Reconnaissance from Tenefelde and Olster told Neumann that the goods were stored in the western side of the building, and that the eastern side was being used as living quarters. So Neumann headed east and approached the door that was propped open at the end of the hall, trying not to let his footsteps creak too much on the wooden floor. It didn't work.

"You don't need to sneak up on me, Sergeant Neumann," he heard Heidfeld call out from the room beyond the door. "I knew someone like you would be coming for me."

The sound of Heidfeld's voice indicated that he was some distance away from the door. Still, Neumann moved deliberately through the doorway, in case there was some kind of trap or Heidfeld had another ally that Neumann was unaware of.

But there was no ambush this time either. The room was a mess; clothes and food were tossed all over the place, and the stink of unwashed prisoners, piss, and rotting food mingled in the air. At the far end of the long room, just before the north wall, were four bunks, the ones they had moved in here a few days ago to protect their goods.

Heidfeld sat with his back to Neumann on one of the lower bunks. His shoulders were hunched over; he looked like a defeated man. Neumann started walking towards him, hoping for the best but realizing he had no idea what to do with Heidfeld when he got him. He remembered his fury over Knaup, and the speech he had given about being merciless like the Russians. But now, facing someone who looked so pitiful, he didn't feel so merciless. Maybe he would just turn Heidfeld over to the Canadians so they could put him in protective custody and the man would live out the rest of the war in ignominy.

But as Neumann got within four metres of the bunk, Heidfeld slowly stood up. Neumann stopped; something didn't feel right. It was too easy.

Heidfeld turned, wild-eyed, and brought up him his right hand to point a pistol at Neumann. A chill went through Neumann's body as he processed the shock of seeing a loaded gun inside the camp.

It was a design he was familiar with, but not the Enfield No. 2 favoured by the Brits as a sidearm in the current war. This was an older pistol, maybe a Webley Mk IV. It had a tendency to jump and didn't have the stopping power of the No. 2, which is why the Brits stopped using them before the onset of this war. But Neumann had seen many of these guns in the trenches, especially in the hands of Germans; they had taken them off the bodies of sentimental Boer War veterans who had brought the pistols with them into combat once more. Sentiment towards weapons from a previous war always had a way of getting you killed in the next one.

But despite its vintage, the pistol in Heidfeld's hand was still a deadly weapon.

Neumann knew that Heidfeld must be very anxious about his standing in the camp to think that he needed a gun to protect himself. Even the Canadians didn't carry rifles into the camp for fear they would be stolen by the prisoners and used against them.

"Where ..." was all Neumann could think to say, his voice trailing away.

"I can get anything I want into this camp; women, drink, morphine, even a gun. That's the kind of power I have," Heidfeld said with a small chuckle.

"Not anymore."

"Maybe," he said with a shrug. "Your crazy stunt with the orchestra was a setback, I'll admit. As is your crackdown on my operation. I could shoot you now, but you surprised me, Sergeant Neumann. And I'm impressed enough to give you one last chance before I shoot."

"A chance to do what?" Neumann asked, trying to keep Heidfeld talking while he thought of a way to distract him. He kept his gaze on Heidfeld's eyes, but watched the gun in his periphery.

"One last chance to partner up with me," Heidfeld said, flashing a charming smile. "You and I shouldn't be adversaries, Neumann; we should be partners. Together we'd control so much of the camp that even the Canadians would be afraid of us."

"I'm not interested in that kind of power," Neumann replied.

"Always the honourable Sergeant Neumann," Heidfeld said, lowering the pistol slightly. Neumann shifted his weight to one foot, planning to slowly step back from Heidfeld.

"That's not going to work in Germany after the war. People like you are going to need to be more flexible for us to move forward, or you'll be left behind," Heidfeld said, making a point of raising the gun and jerking it in Neumann's direction. The sergeant froze. "Or be killed in the process," Heidfeld added.

"Killing me won't get you anywhere. It'll only anger the Canadians more."

Heidfeld laughed but the gun did not waver. "The Canadians don't care how many of us die in this camp. Mueller, Horcoff, Schlipal … Knaup."

Neumann bristled at the mention of Knaup's name. It was difficult for him to contain his rising anger and to stop himself from rushing Heidfeld because of the casual way he mentioned the doomed corporal's name. But Neumann knew it was a ploy meant to rattle him, so he took a breath, a slow one to mask how effective it had been. But Heidfeld's widening grin showed that he wasn't fooled.

"And what have the Canadians done? Absolutely nothing," he continued. "Because they *don't* care. We're at war, so a few dead Germans make no difference to them."

"Shots fired with a contraband weapon might."

"Probably," Heidfeld nodded. "They'll raid the camp, turn over every bunk, table, and chair until I let them find it. But they'll do little to find your killer. And even if they do, I'll probably find someone else to pin it on. And in the end, you'll be dead and no one will challenge me in this camp again."

Neumann had to admit that Heidfeld was right, and he saw in the other sergeant's eyes that he was running out of time to escape. Heidfeld was a big fan of dramatic gestures, and especially liked to hear the sound of his own voice. But he was also a pragmatist who knew when it was time to act, and he had said his piece.

Neumann had to act fast if he wanted to survive the night. His ploy was simple: a quick, furtive look to a spot behind Heidfeld as a distraction. He wasn't sure if it would work, but he had to try.

A soldier with years of direct combat experience wouldn't have flinched but, fortunately for Neumann, the staff sergeant wasn't that kind of soldier. He did register the movement of Neumann's eyes and instinctively turned to the side to see if there was someone behind him. Even as he did so, Neumann could tell that Heidfeld realized he had been fooled. But it was enough for Neumann to react.

Unlike his tactic outside the theatre, Neumann did not rush forward. Instead, he turned and started running along the bunks, zigzagging as he did so. It wasn't much of an escape plan, but after years of battle experience, Neumann knew that shooting a moving target, even one at relatively close range, even if someone was a decent shot, was very difficult. Especially when the shooter was under significant stress, as Heidfeld was, and had no experience using the weapon they held.

Still, Heidfeld fired once. The bullet struck a bunk just to the right of Neumann and he felt the bite of the wood slivers a fraction of a second before he heard the blast of the pistol.

"Fuck!" Heidfeld shouted.

Even though basic human instinct would immediately drive a person to move away from the line of fire, Neumann forced himself to run in a straight line for a brief second. Heidfeld fired another shot and the high-pitched whine of a bullet flew just to his left, where he would have been had he not stayed his course. The bullet embedded itself in wall a few yards ahead of Neumann.

He veered towards a window and jumped, wrapping his arms around his torso and tucking his head into his chest. The single pane of glass easily shattered from the impact. He hit the ground feet first, knees flexed, and rolled over like a paratrooper to absorb the jolt of his landing. Still, his body registered several jabs of pain from the shards of glass that had penetrated through his winter jacket and from where his teeth had snapped together, biting through a small section of his tongue. A copper taste filled his mouth. The adrenaline coursing through his body pushed such minor concerns aside, but it also heightened the fight and flee instinct in him.

But combat had taught Neumann to quell that impulse and to use the adrenaline for clarity. Time seemed to slow, and Neumann took in his surroundings before jumping into a decision of what to do next.

He heard Heidfeld swear and then his footsteps coming towards the window. At that instant, Neumann registered the distant shouts of Canadians reacting to the shots from Heidfeld's weapon. Lights from the nearby towers flew in their direction, searching for the source. The sound of the shots had probably echoed off the barracks and the mess buildings to the south, so it would be difficult for the Canadians to pinpoint their location. But a gunshot inside the camp was unheard of since the camp had opened, so their response would be quick.

Neumann knew he had time to flee to a nearby barracks building and hide out until the ruckus faded. He also knew that Heidfeld was probably thinking the same, that Neumann had escaped into the night to get away from the gun. And the thought of this kind of retreat flashed for a moment in Neumann's mind. But he instantly dismissed it.

It was not a time to retreat. He had to act and end this battle tonight or face a longer, more costly one until the end of the war. His body immediately responded to this decision and less than a second after coming to his feet from his paratrooper roll, Neumann jumped back to the outside wall of the classroom and crouched to the left of the window he had just crashed through. He listened as Heidfeld's footsteps came closer, his muscles tightening, waiting for the right moment to strike.

As an adjutant to a commander, Heidfeld had been under fire in his time in North Africa but didn't have as much direct experience in combat as Neumann. He had never been tasked with trying to take an enemy position or defend one of their own the way Neumann, Aachen, and his squad had almost every single day of the war since it started.

So he did not take the precautions known to those who had faced the enemy. Instead of approaching the now bare window with caution, as someone in battle should, he stuck his head and torso out to see where Neumann had fled. It was only a second, but it was enough.

In one fluid motion, Neumann leapt to a standing position, grabbed handfuls of Heidfeld's uniform, and yanked. Shock and surprise exploded across the staff sergeant's face as Neumann rose up in front of him but he was pulled through the window before he had time to react, his forehead hitting the top of the wooden frame in the process.

Neumann fell backwards, flipping Heidfeld over in a somersault and then releasing his hold so that the staff sergeant landed hard and flat across his back, the wind knocked out of him. He grunted, but with no breath he made little noise. The gun flew out of his grip, landing harmlessly in the snow several metres away. Blood seeped from the gash on his forehead.

Neumann jumped onto Heidfeld, and knocked him senseless with several open-handed slaps across his face and head. Heidfeld went limp. Neumann stood up and pressed his boot on the man's neck, then looked around for the gun. It was about three metres away, the heat from the recently fired barrel melting the snow around it.

Neumann lifted his foot from Heidfeld's neck but gave him a quick couple of kicks in the ribs to keep him down. He ran over to grab the gun and quickly returned to pin Heidfeld to the ground.

He pointed the pistol at the staff sergeant, who was semi-conscious and moaning in pain. Blood was now seeping from his mouth and nose. Neumann threw some snow on Heidfeld to get his attention. He sputtered a bit and opened a swollen eye to look at Neumann and the gun pointed at his head.

"Fuck you," Heidfeld said. "You won't kill me."

Neumann chuckled and nodded. "You're right, I won't."

A look of smug satisfaction came over Heidfeld's face. But it turned into fear and horror when Neumann grabbed his right hand and pulled it up towards the gun.

The staff sergeant struggled so Neumann pistol-whipped him a couple of times, breaking his resistance for a moment. In that time, he forced the gun into Heidfeld's hand and pressed the barrel to the base of the staff sergeant's chin. Heidfeld's eyes went wide and he twisted to try to break away but did not have the strength to free himself. His left arm slapped at Neumann but the blows were too weak to be effective.

Without a weapon, Heidfeld was no match in strength against Neumann. No one in the camp was. Maybe Aachen, but they had never had the chance to determine that.

Neumann forced Heidfeld's finger into the trigger, breaking the man's resistance by breaking his finger. Heidfeld groaned in pain and the sound attracted the Canadians. "Over there," someone shouted in English from a few hundred metres way.

Neumann didn't have much time, but he still slowly pulled back on the hammer. Heidfeld's eyes snapped open in fear as he heard the noise.

"You won't—" Heidfeld began to say.

The gun fired.

38.

The crack of the shot attracted more shouts from the Canadians. Neumann could hear the sound of their boots crunching in the snow, coming much closer.

There was no way he could make it to the barracks without being seen. They would catch him, then find Heidfeld's body and charge him with murder.

He'd probably hang.

So Neumann decided to go the other way. He crawled away from Heidfeld, back towards the wall of the classroom, and pulled himself up through the open window.

Once inside, he walked quickly towards the bunks, pulling out his lighter. He snapped it open and lit the flame. He adjusted it so the flame grew larger and then held it against the edge of one of the mattresses. After a second, the material caught fire and the flame spread across the surface.

Neumann made to move out of the room, tossing his still-burning lighter onto another mattress. That one caught fire as well and by the time Neumann had left the room, the wood from the bunks had started to burn. Soon the fire would spread to the walls of the building and there would be no stopping it; all of the contraband would be destroyed.

After checking that the coast was clear, Neumann left the building, heading north towards the hospital. He moved quickly on the path, trying to stay below the level of the drifts along the outside edges. When a tower light drifted in his direction, he dropped and crawled on his belly until the light moved away. He moved as fast as he could, the same way he crawled and scrambled through the enemy trenches when he escaped after killing those four Brits in 1917.

Although it felt like it was taking him forever to get to the hospital, he knew he was making good time. And he hoped the Canadians' reaction to Heidfeld with a pistol would be too powerful of a scene to leave. And though some like Major MacKay would question whether Heidfeld killed himself, the same way they questioned whether General Horcoff did as well, the presence of the gun in the hands of a German prisoner would be more important. How and where he got the gun would be the focus of any investigation, rather than the death of a German.

And then there was the fire. In order to prevent it from spreading to other buildings, the Canadians would probably need the help of the prisoners. Many of them would come out to stop the fire from spreading to the buildings where they had classes, workshops, and other recreational pursuits.

This chaos would make it even more difficult for the Canadians to figure out why Heidfeld was dead. In their zeal to find out how the pistol got into the camp, they would probably assume the easiest answer about Heidfeld. At least that's what Neumann hoped.

The door to the hospital wasn't locked, so Neumann slipped in, quickly closing the door behind him. Before any of the orderlies discovered him, he made his way to Knaup's room, removing his coat and dropping it into a laundry hamper in the hallway. But even if one of the orderlies spotted him, they would say nothing. Someone would clean the jacket without question.

But no one spotted him and he made it to Knaup's room. Knaup lay in bed, still in a coma, still breathing shallowly but probably not for long. Neumann sighed and turned away. There was little he could do for Knaup except what he had just done.

In a cabinet in the corner, Neumann found a first aid kit and gingerly removed the splinters and a couple bits of glass from his face and neck. He cleaned the wounds with some alcohol. He didn't look great, but his new wounds were small and seemed to blend in with his existing bruises.

Later on, he might be questioned about them by the Canadians, but then, so would many of the other prisoners like Konrad and anyone else who had suffered injuries in the recent battle. Or in fighting the fire. But what had happened was a matter between Germans, not the Canadians. He would say nothing. None of them, even those who had supported Heidfeld, would say anything.

Neumann turned and looked at Knaup again and realized that there was something he could do for the corporal. He searched the cabinet again and found a pencil and a pad of paper, probably used by the orderlies or Dr. Kleinjeld to take notes.

Neumann sat on the chair next to Knaup's bed and started writing a letter to Knaup's family, telling them of their son's death and the sorrow he shared with them. But he also praised Knaup as a good German, a good soldier who until his death, did his duty to his country, and most importantly, to his squad and the men in the camp he agreed to protect.

If the Canadians came looking in the hospital, they would see him just as he was: a sergeant sitting at the bedside of one of his wounded squad members, writing a letter to the man's family.

And as he wrote, Neumann hoped that he had just killed the last man he would have to kill in this goddamn war.

The Traitors of Camp 133

A Sergeant Neumann Mystery
by Wayne Arthurson

Captain Mueller is dead. Hanged, apparently, by his own hand. But ex-police officer and war hero Sergeant August Neumann doesn't think it's quite so simple. How could it be with black-shirts, legionnaires, and communist sympathisers vying for control of the camp?

Now Sergeant Neumann must navigate these treacherous cliques to find the truth while under the watchful eyes of his Canadian captors.

The Traitors of Camp 133 is a murder mystery that delivers: we believe and care about the characters, we take wrong turns, we grieve. Wayne Arthurson wraps his mystery in a fascinating subculture: German POWs in a Southern Alberta camp shortly after the Allies invade Normandy. It's a great read.

—Todd Babiak, bestselling author of
Come Barbarians and *Son of France*

The Traitors of Camp 133 / $16.95
ISBN: 9780888015877
Ravenstone